Money, Murder & Memories

Malik D. Rice

Lock Down Publications and Ca$h
Presents
Money, Murder & Memories
A Novel by *Malik D. Rice*

Money, Murder & Memories

Lock Down Publications
P.O. Box 944
Stockbridge, Ga 30281

Copyright 2020 by Malik D. Rice
Money, Murder & Memories

Lock Down Publications
Like our page on Facebook: Lock Down Publications @
www.facebook.com/lockdownpublications.ldp
Cover design and layout by: **Dynasty Cover Me**
Book interior design by: **Shawn Walker**
Edited by: **Shamika Smith**

Stay Connected with Us!

Text **LOCKDOWN** to 22828 to stay up-to-date with new releases, sneak peaks, contests and more...

Thank you!

Submission Guideline.

Submit the first three chapters of your completed manuscript to ldpsubmissions@gmail.com, subject line: Your book's title. The manuscript must be in a .doc file and sent as an attachment. Document should be in Times New Roman, double spaced and in size 12 font. Also, provide your synopsis and full contact information. If sending multiple submissions, they must each be in a separate email.

Have a story but no way to send it electronically? You can still submit to LDP/Ca$h Presents. Send in the first three chapters, written or typed, of your completed manuscript to:

LDP: Submissions Dept
P.O. Box 944
Stockbridge, Ga 30281

DO NOT send original manuscript. Must be a duplicate.

Provide your synopsis and a cover letter containing your full contact information.

Thanks for considering LDP and Ca$h Presents.

Malik D. Rice

Chapter 1
~ Part 1 ~
Rondo

I bent down to pull my eighteen-year-old cousin, Jay, off of his latest victim. He was a natural live wire that didn't know how to control his quick temper, which is why he was on the run for an aggregated assault. It was times like this where I felt like all the help that I was giving him was being taken for granted. He'd obviously never learns.

He was midnight black with a lanky build, standing two feet shorter than me at 6-feet even. He was a very difficult individual who didn't listen to anyone but me, and that was only most of the time.

"Come on, Jay. You trippin', bro!" I barked trying to get him far away from the unconscious man who laid on the ground with a bloody face.

A crowd of onlookers gathered around with their phones out recording the incident that would surely be on social media in the next few minutes. I looked around at them in disgust as I ushered Jay over to my silver 2012 Impala.

"Every time I turn around, you into some shit. I take care of you. I make sure you got a place to stay. All I ever asked for you to do was sit your ass down, and somehow that's too much to ask from you. What the problem?" I asked not trying to hide the extreme irritation in my voice.

"This ain't even got nothing to do with me. I hopped on that nigga because I overheard him talking shit about you! You need to watch your back out here because it's a lot of niggas around here that don't like how you flew past them like that. I can see the hate in a lot of them niggas' eyes when you around."

Jay's words cut deep into my mind as I drove out of Flat Shoals Crossing Apartments onto Flat Shoals Road. I couldn't say another word to him about the previous incident because I did like the fact that he defended my name behind my back, and I too had seen the hate in niggas eyes whenever I came around now. I knew a lot of niggas were threatened by my success, but that wasn't my concern. It was my job to get money, and take care of mines, not to cater to the next man's feelings.

A few short minutes later, we were pulling up in front of my house. My mother left me her house when she passed, so I moved in and took care of the house that she worked too hard to earn and keep.

"There goes the love of your life," Jay informed with a smile that showed the spacious gap between his two front teeth.

I laid my eyes on the silver '96 Mustang and let out a knowing sigh. It was Chyanne. She was literally the worst-and-best thing that ever happened to me. The worst, because she cheated on me with one of my partners and broke my heart into pieces during a critical time in my life, and the best because I took that same pain that she caused me and turned it into extreme motivation. That same motivation made me the man I was today.

I gave Jay a knowing glance. "Fuck you, Jay. Go dust that lawnmower off and tighten the yard up."

The humor left Jay's face in a millisecond as he now stared at me with a face hard as stone.

"You don't scare me, lil' nigga. You know the rules. You stay here rent-free as long as you keep the house up-to-par. Now go handle the business. I'm about to send this girl on about her day," I said as I parked my car in my driveway.

Chyanne was parked on the curb in front of my house leaning on her hood with her arm's folded and snuggled up in a tight-fitting H&M jean jacket. "I never understood why you liked standing outside in the cold," I said while thinking back on the countless times she made me stand in the cold with her.

She shrugged her shoulders. "It's not cold, it's chilly, but it feels good to me. Gives me a peace of mind."

I shivered slightly as a cold wind blew past us. I shoved my hands deeper into the pockets of my Ralph Lauren hoodie. "That's nice, but another thing I don't understand is why you're here. You must've left something in the house that I don't know about."

She averted eye contact as she shook her head in disagreement.

"So, what is it? I know you not here to see me," I stated.

She made eye contact once again. "I really am here to see you, Rondo. You won't answer any of my messages, so I had to pull up."

"Shawty, I loved you more than anybody on this earth. You were all I had in this world after my mama died. I gave you my all, and you repaid me with a knife in the back... Ain't shit for us to talk about," I stated firmly.

I watched as the tears formed in her eyes and began to escape down her face. I knew for a fact that she wasn't innocent, but she looked so fragile and harmless to me at that moment. She was a master manipulator, and I had to be very careful around her. She was toxic, and I'd be damned if I got sucked back into her bullshit.

She wore her weave long just how I liked it with her edges gelled down stylishly. Her big lips were glossed to perfection, and her thick curves showed perfectly in her tight clothing. I couldn't even be mad at my homeboy for having sex with her.

"I made *one* mistake and you go to tripping. Nobody's perfect, Rondo. How many times have I caught you cheating?" she asked sassily with a hand on her small waist.

"A few, but you didn't know none of them hoes. You fucked one of the niggas that I used to chill with every day. A nigga I used to call my brother. Ain't no telling how long y'all was fucking behind my back and laughed at me like I was stupid." My anger began to rise just thinking about the deceitful actions of two people that I once trusted with my life.

"That was the first and only time, Rondo. I swear," she promised seriously.

"One-time way too many. You're wasting your time, Chyanne. There could *never* be a 'me and you' again. You was never Loyal 4Eva. You're dead to me, shawty," I informed before turning around and walked towards my house. She called after me, but I kept on walking. She didn't have a hold on me anymore. I was free.

Chapter 2

Later on that night, I woke Jay up so he could ride with me to handle this late-night business. The days of me running with packs of niggas were long gone. It was hard for me to trust people those days, so I'd been moving very differently during the past few months.

Ever since I stopped doing drugs, partying, hanging around a lot of niggas and started focusing, laying low, and distancing myself away from crowds, I'd been prospering like never before. If I would've known that a change in work-ethic and lifestyle would've made me a rich man, I would've done it a *long* time ago.

"What you gon' do if I get caught?" Jay asked suddenly from the passenger's seat as I eased onto the highway ramp of I-20 West on Flat Shoals.

"Where the hell that come from?" I asked curiously. He never asked questions like that, so it honestly threw me for a loop.

"I'm just saying. I've been noticing how you ain't been kicking it with nobody but me since that shit that happened with Chyanne, so I was just over here wondering what you gon' do without me," Jay said matter-a-factly.

I had to think about that because he was right. Nobody outside of himself could tell you what went on inside of my daily life because I had shut everyone out, so his question made sense. "I mean, I hope you never do get caught, but shit happens. So, if you do, I guess I'm just gon' have to find somebody else I trust to watch my back."

He burst out laughing at my answer. "Nigga, you don't trust nobody but me."

"Yeah, I know. That's the whole problem."

***

About fifty minutes later, we were inside of a high-tech mini-mansion and walking through a house party that was turnt up. Rich kids from all around the metro Atlanta area were in attendance and ready to party like it was their last day on earth. It looked like something out of the movie *Project X*. It was literally a zoo.

The house belonged to Cliff. Cliff was one of those rich white kids who did things just for the thrill, and selling cocaine was definitely one of them. I don't know which gangster movies he'd been watching in his early teenage years, but for some reason, he had the strong urge to be a high-end drug dealer. I didn't have the slightest problem with that because he bought two bricks a week from me at $45,000 apiece. That was unheard of.

I saw him before he saw me. He stood over a very attractive Asian woman as she laid backward half-naked on the kitchen counter while he licked chocolate syrup off of her flat stomach. Onlookers cheered him on as he licked up the last little bit of syrup by her breast.

"Wooooooooooo!" Cliff roared in triumph as he stood all the way up with his long blonde hair all in his face. He was short, chubby, and super friendly. Not your ideal image of a drug dealer.

He laid his eyes on me and his smile broadened as he made his way over to where I stood with Jay sticking to me like a parasite. "What's the special occasion?" I asked as he came within earshot. He threw parties on a normal basis, but this was over-the-top. It had to be a celebration.

"One of my buddy's 20th birthday bash, bro! You should stick around! This isn't shit! We're just getting warmed up!" he suggested, excitedly.

I gave him a knowing look.

"Yeah, I know! Strictly businesses with you... Follow me!"

He led the way to his upstairs bedroom. The party stretched all throughout the house. He even had to kick a group of people out of his room, so we could deal privately.

"Business has been booming this way! I might have to up my shipment soon. A lot of new clientele to be served," Cliff informed proudly from his walk-in closet while entering the code to his digital safe.

Jay and I exchanged amused glances. Cliff got off on shit like this. He didn't need to sell drugs any more than I needed to be with Chyanne, but he still did it because it made him feel more interesting. He knew what I was about and he knew what I represented, so dealing with me made him official. All he wanted was to be taken seriously, and most street niggas weren't willing to do that because he wasn't from the trenches. However, I took him seriously, which is why he continued to spend his dollars with me and *only* me.

"You know I got an unlimited supply of this shit, so just let me know ahead of time. I can have the shit ready for you... You're going to have to start meeting me halfway too. I'm not about to keep driving all the way out here. Too many police," I informed as he walked out of the closet with a pillowcase filled with the usual fifty-dollar bills.

"Yeah, I understand. It's no problem, bro. Just name the location, and I'll be there for the next drop," said Cliff while handing Jay the pillowcase. I took the single wrapped bricks out of my Bally book bag and placed them on his bed.

I grabbed the bag from Jay, dumped the contents into my bag, and tossed the pillowcase back to Cliff, who caught it with his left hand. "Nice doing business with you. I'll make sure you get my new number when I change it." I changed my business number every four days as a security precaution.

Cliff smirked knowingly and reached his hand out for a shake. "Same time next week, bro."

After I shook his hand, he extended his hand out to, Jay, who looked at him with the same grimace he kept on his face most of the time.

"Yeah, I know. No handshakes from you. I had to try though," Cliff joked, but no one laughed except him.

"Hold it down, Cliff. I'll see you next week fool," I stated before leading the way out of the house.

Chapter 3

After leaving Cliff's house, we treated ourselves to a late breakfast at IHOP because we had a long weekend ahead of ourselves. Cliff was the only client that I trusted to deliver to, but for the rest, it was a totally different story. We spent the majority of our time motel hopping serving niggas from all over.

It was a drought on uncut cocaine in Georgia, and I was one of the few people who barely stepped on my product. Ever since 2-Tall fell out with Malina and the Cartel went up on Dilluminati's prices, shit got ugly in Georgia since we were supplying sixty percent of the state's cocaine.

Most niggas found it logical to step on their product in order to maintain the same juicy profit they were used to, but I found it smarter to maintain quality and take a cut in profit to keep the customers happy. It was working out wonderfully for me.

A uniquely indistinct Latin woman I've come very familiar with came into view and helped herself to a seat at our booth. Her name was Mrs. Lopez, and she was a professional money launderer. I'd been dealing with her for a little over a month, and thanks to her, I was already sitting on just over two-hundred thousand dollars in legitimate funds. She handled money well, didn't charge too much for her services, and asked *zero* questions.

"I see you're a busy man, Mr. Rondo," she stated in a form of greeting.

I slid my Bally bag, filled with the $90,000 I got from Cliff, across the floor with my foot. "As long as I'm busy, you're busy. That's a good thing ain't it?"

She bent down and picked the back up. "Yes, it is. Enjoy the rest of your night gentlemen," she said before getting up from the booth and leaving the restaurant.

"I don't know about her, bro," Jay informed while watching Mrs. Lopez walk away in her stylish pantsuit. "I wouldn't trust the bitch like that."

I took a few sips of my coffee, then looked up at Jay. "If anybody knows, you know that I don't trust a soul, nigga. If that bitch even thought about crossing me, all twelve of her family members gon' come up missing faster than she can spell *taco*, and that's something she knows."

Jay chucked while shaking his small head slowly.

"What?" I asked with a raised eyebrow.

"It's just... Crazy to me how you got everything figured out all of a sudden. Just four months ago, we was in the same boat, now you done turned into a whole mob boss that fast," he stated seriously.

I shrugged my shoulders with a blank expression. "Maybe my mama was right. Maybe I've always been smart, just needed to embrace the shit."

I remember my mother's words like it was just yesterday.

I walked into the hospital room to the horrible sight of my mother. She'd always been so energized and full of life, so to see her like this wasn't good for my health. It did something wicked to my soul.

She laid in her hospital bed staring at me blankly as I walked into the room with a variety of different flowers and balloons that I sat on the table across from her bed by the window.

I grabbed the chair from the corner of the room and dragged it up to her bed so I could be close to her. She reached her frail hand out for mines, and I grabbed it with a light grip. "How you feeling, beautiful?"

"How you think I'm feeling, boy? It's all good though because I lived a decent life. I just regret the fact that I didn't live it to the fullest," she vented matter-a-factly.

"It's all good, ma. It's still a chance that you can shake this shit," I said because I didn't know what else to say. We both knew that was a dream.

She licked her chapped lips and gazed at me knowingly. "Anyways... Like I was saying. That's the only thing I regret, and I don't want you to end up like me. I want you to live your life to the fullest, baby... Get your priorities straight and distance yourself from them lame ass niggas you've been hanging with, and I promise you'll prosper. You're a smart kid, baby. Embrace that shit and stop selling yourself short. Show the world your potential."

We set up camp at a low-key motel out on Wesley Chapel Road. It was almost half-past five, and the sun would reveal itself soon. It was a fresh day, but we didn't feel fresh because we didn't get any sleep. That's the life we lived. Late night, early morning. Shit, sometimes we didn't get any sleep at all, and today was a prime example.

As soon as we got into the room, Jay took the PlayStation 4 out of his Nike gym bag and hooked it up to the 40-inch flat-screen that was mounted to the wall. While he was getting it situated, I hopped on the phone to make a dozen calls to dudes who'd already placed their orders. As soon as the last call was placed, I laid back on the bed fully clothed, closed my eyes, and drifted off to sleep in a matter of minutes.

About fifty minutes after I drifted off to sleep, I was awakened by Jay, who held my ringing phone in his hand outstretched to me. I grabbed the phone and answered it groggily. I told them what room I was in, hung up, and sat up on the bed while releasing a monstrous yawn. All the late nights and early mornings over the past few months were surely catching up with me, but I couldn't complain because I was getting rich in the process.

I guess yawns were really contagious because Jay released one a few seconds after me while taking a seat over on his bed. He parked his Mac-10 on his lap before unpausing the game.

"You been to sleep?" I asked as I took a brick of cocaine out of my gym bag before sliding it back under my bed.

Jay just shook his head without taking his eyes off of the TV. "That lil' nap in the car and that coffee was enough for me. I'll be good until later on."

"Imagine having a few years run like this," I said.

He laughed at the thought. "We gon' have bags under our eyes like our granddaddy."

A knock came from the door breaking up our conversation. Jay played his role by pausing the game and trying to answer the door for our company, but I told him to keep playing because I somewhat trusted this person. It wasn't that I knew him well enough or anything, I just got a good vibe from him when he came to shop.

I got up and answered the door for OG Hitman and a few of his lil' homies. He was a big homie over a wild Blood set called ZooKrew that was growing by the day. "What's up, young nigga? You look like shit," he informed bluntly before walking past me into the room with his two youngins in tow.

I closed the door and followed. "Just need some sleep, that's all."

"Sleep gon' come, just keep working for now. You doing good things out here," Hitman advised while standing at the end of the walkway while I walked to the bed to grab the product for him.

I handed him the product and one of his men handed me a wad full of cash as usual. There was no need for either of us to check our shit because we knew that it was all good. We'd gained an understanding over time.

"I'll be in touch in a few days," he informed before letting himself out.

I hopped in the shower, changed my clothes, and went back to sleep. The rest of the day consisted of short naps, transactions, cold pizza, and video games. The drugs went faster than the last time. It was time for me to up my order from the plug. I needed more drugs.

Malik D. Rice

Chapter 4

The only time that you wouldn't find me with Jay was when I went to visit my stash spot. I trusted him with my life, but unfortunately, I didn't trust him with the location to hundreds of thousands of dollars in cash.

I gave portions of my money to Mrs. Lopez and I kept the rest hidden in a U-Haul storage room out in Conyers, Georgia. Of course, I didn't just have a square pile of money sitting in the middle of the floor like you may have seen in some movies. This was real life. I had to always think ahead and be precautious, so the storage room was filled with old furniture, and I had money stashed in different places.

I opened the lock on the garage door with a key and closed it behind myself. I flipped the light switch and looked around the room. I don't think anyone would ever predict that a fortune was stashed in the old furniture.

I walked over to one of the small couches and took all of the cushions off of it. Then I reached down and pulled out the sofa bed where $50,000 was hidden. I grabbed the large bundle of money, that was wrapped in saran and put the couch back together. After the cushions were replaced, I took a seat on the couch with a heavy huff.

I was still tired. I wanted to lay down on the couch and catch a quick nap, but I had business to handle, so I settled for a quick meditation session. I looked down at the money that laid on the couch, and it took me back to a visit I had with my mother on her deathbed.

My mother was asleep when I came to check on her this time, but the nurse let me sit with her after promising that I wouldn't wake her. I kept my promise, but my mother woke up on her own. I

21

was watching an old episode of "Jerry Springer" that was playing on the television when I heard her weak voice. "Heyyy son. What you doing here?" Usually, she would try to sit up in the bed and I would stop her, but lately, she wasn't having the energy for that anymore. She just laid there on her side looking at me.

"I'm checking on my mama. What else? Hard to enjoy my life out there knowing you laid up in here all alone."

She sighed loudly. "Listen to me, boy... I was adopted by a woman that was adopted herself. When she died that left me nobody... Until I had you. Now unfortunately for you, you're about to suffer the same fate, but I refuse to leave you with nothing like my mother did me. After I'm gone, you gon' get a $50,000 settlement. Fuck coming to visit me and all this sap ass shit. I'm at peace. I lived my life. If you really want to make me happy, you gon' take that money, and you gon' do something with it."

"What?" I didn't even know she had life insurance on herself, that was the furthest thing from my mind.

"Rondo, shut up and listen, boy! I ain't gon' lie like I didn't have high hopes for you. I wanted you to be a doctor, lawyer, or even a dentist, or fireman. I wanted anything for you but those streets. However, you wanted the streets, so it was nothing I could do about that... I sat there and watched you play around in those streets taking penitentiary chances for peanuts. I sat there and watched you hustling backwards for years... If you really love me, you gon' take that settlement and be the biggest drug dealer you can be. If you gon' do something, be the best at what you do, baby."

I opened my eyes and wiped the oncoming tears that I felt coming. I had to be strong and keep pushing. My mother was in heaven watching my every move and I had to continue making her proud.

Money, Murder & Memories

***

Stevo was the top Mafioso in my camp. He supplied the rest of the Mafioso's, who then supplied their Mobsters. After the first month of my mother's death, I was awarded Mafioso stripes from Stevo. He saw how I was handling business and he began helping me by fronting the same amount of product that I came to buy. We weren't personal friends; our relationship was all business. I knew he had my best interest at heart, so I respected and saluted him to the fullest.

He stayed in a nice Buckhead apartment, but spent most of his time in the hood at his other spot in Flat Shoals Crossing. That's where he conducted business. Usually, he'd stay holed up inside, so I was surprised to see him leaning on the hood of his BMW surrounded by a handful of Mobsters, who seemed excited to be around him.

I parked a few spaces over from him and walked over there with Jay beside me. "Wassup, bro? I see you done finally came out for some sunlight," I greeted as I dapped Stevo up.

"Yeah, it's too warm of a day for it to be December. That global warming a muthafucka," he stated.

I glanced at the nosey Mobsters around, then set my eyes back on Stevo. "Want me to come back a lil' later on?"

Stevo shook his odd-shaped head. "Nah. Give the duffle bag to Jay and have him take it upstairs. The product will be here when we get back."

"Get back?" I asked with a raised brow.

Stevo nodded. "Me and you about to take a lil' trip... Jay gon' hold it down in my spot until we get back."

Stevo told Jay to take the duffle bag full of money he was carrying and take it upstairs to his spot. Stevo's cousins watched over the spot, so Jay would just have to sit around playing video games with them until we got back.

Just like Jay said the other day, I could see and feel the envy in the Mobsters that stood around watching me hop into the car with Stevo for a *special ride*. I was once on the bottom scraping the surface with them. When I was broke, they seemed happy, but now that I'd elevated past them, I could sense the anger even though some of them tried not to show it.

"You handle that shit good," Stevo complimented while driving out of the neighborhood.

I put on my seatbelt after watching him strap on his. "What you mean?"

"The envy... I can tell you sense it, but you don't let it bother you. That's how it's supposed to be."

"Yeah, you know how that shit goes... Where we going anyway? You ain't never took me on no special ride before," I asked and then stated.

He glanced over at me with a smug grin. "We're going to see the Don."

Chapter 5

Allo was the Don over our camp. I'd seen him once before at a block party and never knew that the short, stocky, brown skin man with no jewelry was our Don until he made a speech letting everybody know that he was the new Don over our camp. He explained that he would be taking the place of our previous Don, Spider, who'd been missing for weeks. Nobody in our camp but Stevo has seen Allo since that day.

Stevo drove to a nice little neighborhood in Cabbage Town by Grant Park. It sat behind a small shopping plaza. It only consisted of five elegant stone houses that were lined up side-by-side. When you went into the alley behind the plaza, there was a dirt road that looked like it led into a patch of woods. But once you took that right turn on the road, the woods opened up to the small neighborhood.

The houses were connected to each other, but they all had separate driveways and backyards. Stevo parked behind Allo's Alfa Romeo truck and turned the car off. "Just walk up to the door and ring the doorbell. He'll answer."

I had asked Stevo why we were going to see the Don, and he just shrugged his shoulders. He was just following orders to bring me to Allo. "You staying in the car?" I tried to hide my uneasiness, but the smirk on Stevo's face told me that it wasn't working. He saw right through me.

"Yeah, nigga. I'll be right here when you come out."

I opened the door and made my way up the driveway to the front door of the house. I didn't have to ring the doorbell because the door opened as I approached the door. Allo stood there holding the door open looking excited to see me like he was inviting family inside. "Rondo, wassup lil' nigga?"

I dapped him up and stepped into the house as he waved me inside. "Trying to figure out what I did to get summoned by the Don himself," I answered truthfully.

"Come pop-a-squat with me for a lil' minute." He led the way through the house.

It wasn't overly extravagant like I expected. It was decorated like a regular middle-class home. R&B music played smoothly from a speaker in the living room. He led me into the kitchen where he had his dinner cooking on the stove. "I'm whipping up this fully-loaded spaghetti and turkey salad. I would invite you to eat dinner with me, but you've been a busy man these past few months."

I nodded my head up-and-down while standing there awkwardly watching him stir the noodles in the pot.

"When you pulled up on Stevo with that fifty-thousand a few months ago, he put you on hold because he wanted to check with me first before supplying you with that kind of work. I told him to give it to you because money is money at the end of the day. Who am I to deprive the next man of his shot at greatness? I kept an eye on you ever since then, and I can't even lie, shawty... You done shocked the fuck out of me. Your work ethic and dedication to the hustle is superior. You don't see that out here every day."

"I appreciate that big bro. I'm just trying to be the best I can be out here," I responded honestly. I knew I was doing good for myself, but for the Don himself to pull my coattail was *major*.

Allo sat the large fork down that he used to stir the noodles with and picked up a sleek knife before walking over to the counter where he started to chop up a large chunk of uncooked turkey. "That's an understatement. You went from a zero to a hero real quick. You done made legend status, which is both a blessing and a curse in your case."

"What you mean?" I really wanted to tell him to cut to the chase, but I knew better. Made-men in Dilluminati were notorious for their sacred wise-guy speeches and took it as a sign of disrespect if interrupted, especially by one of their own.

"Be real with me. How much money did you make these past few months?" he asked curiously.

"Enough," I retorted swiftly.

He put the knife down, turned around facing me, and leaned on the counter with his arms crossed. "I like that. Never let a nigga count your pockets, but unfortunately, I've been keeping track of your money. If you ain't been spending too much money, which I don't think you have, you should be a couple hundred thousand dollars short of a million. And after this flip, you'll be a million-aire. A muthafuckin' millionaire in just under four months! That's unheard of. You climbing up the ladder *fast* young nigga. How does it feel?"

I shrugged my shoulders. "It's alright. I mean, it ain't nothing how I thought it would be. I always thought when a nigga got money, he got happier. But so far, it's only making a nigga more paranoid."

"As you should be. You'll survive in this game a long time that way, but back to what I was saying... You're climbing up the ladder super-fast, and that's a good thing. I love to see a young nigga prosper, but the only problem that you got is that you racing up the wrong ladder."

I fixed my mouth to say something, but he cut me off with an index finger. "Keep an open mind right now, and be grateful, because I don't have to be keeping it so real with you right now. Shit, I don't have to explain myself period, but I feel that you deserve that much. Right now, you're already competition for Stevo. Within a year's time, you'll become competition for me, and that's what's being prevented here. Long story short, this camp ain't big enough for the both of us."

I could feel several emotions brewing inside of me as he painted the picture for me. Confusion, anger, and fear, all boiling in the same pot. I didn't know how to feel, or what to say. I just stood there staring at him intensely.

"Calm down!" he insisted with a trace of humor in his voice. "I'm not gon' get you whacked or nothing like that. I got too much respect for you and you got too much potential, so I got something else in mind."

"Like what?" I desperately wanted to hear what he had up his sleeve, but I played it as cool.

"Masio got a cousin out in North Carolina who goes by the name of Swagg. Swagg is an Underboss in a city out there called Fayetteville. He called Masio complaining about how one of his Don's had just got caught up in a murder case from years back, and he didn't really have anybody else qualified enough to take his spot. Masio and I have been cool since middle school and never lost touch. I called him personally to address another issue when he started venting to me about Swagg's situation, and it was then that a bright idea popped up in my head."

Chapter 6

Two weeks later, I stood in front of the full-length mirror in my room's closet and stared at myself. My skin was a light almond tone that made me look like I was glowing in the sun. I had an athletic body that wasn't full of tattoos like most of the niggas I used to run with. I only had a single red-and-blue DG tattoo below my left eye because it was mandatory.

I ran a hand through my wild curly temped 'fro and smiled at myself showing the new, permanent, white-gold diamond grill I just got a few days ago. It was a present to myself for all the hard work I'd put in over the past few months.

After my mother's funeral, I wore nothing but black clothing until now. I'd been shopping the whole weekend for a brand-new wardrobe. From now on, I'd be draped in nothing but white designer apparel. Although Jay didn't understand why I was giving him all my black clothes and switching to white, he didn't complain. Who would?

I put a Gucci sweater over my head as I walked out of the closet and looked around my empty room. I donated all the furniture in the house except for a few sentimental pieces that I had mailed to my new destination along with all the new furniture I'd bought.

It was time for me to say goodbye to Atlanta forever. This was a new chapter in my life.

Jay and I took turns driving through the night in my new snow white 2015 Hellcat Charger. It was another present to myself. Out of my entire twenty-four years of living, I'd only taken a few trips outside of Georgia. I would've never, in a million years, saw myself moving outside of Georgia for good.

Allo left me no choice, but I took his advice and kept an open mind about the situation. I could look at it like I was being run out of my own city, but then again, I could also look at it like I was being offered a bigger opportunity. I was coming out here to North Carolina to be a made-man and made-men in Dilluminati were treated like Gods, so I couldn't too much complain. The only challenge I would have is adapting to the new environment.

It was 8:00 AM when we made it to the city of Fayetteville. The only thing I knew about the city was Fort Bragg. It was the biggest army base in the country. Other than that, I would just have to learn as I went.

I had the address to my new house. It belonged to Redd. He was the last Don over Fayetteville's drug camp. His family inherited all his riches, but the house was given to him by Swagg, so it was considered DG property. That's why I was moving in and making it my own. When the GPS told me to make a right turn into the small neighborhood, I smiled.

It sort of reminded me of Allo's neighborhood. It wasn't as low-key, but it was definitely a super-small luxurious neighborhood. Instead of five, this neighborhood only had four houses. They were all identical, but they weren't connected. There was one big wraparound driveway that covered all four houses, but they all still had separate driveways of their own that were connected to that.

The GPS told me that my house was on the far end where a group of people lounged in front. Swagg told me he'd be waiting for me at my destination, so I wasn't alarmed. I parked my car in the driveway and got out with Jay. The sun was shining, but it wasn't as warm up here as it was in Georgia. Seems that North Carolina was having a normal winter. I was going to have to order some more winter gear online as soon as I got the chance.

A heavyset dark-skinned man, who put you in the mind of the rapper, Jadakiss with hair, walked up the driveway to greet us. It had to be Swagg. "Glad you found your way." He looked at my car and chuckled. "I see y'all riding low-key."

I looked back at my sparkling new ride in confusion. "Low-key? You should've seen how I was riding before."

Swagg pointed at the rest of the driveways filled with at least two foreign cars apiece. "We like to show out around this way." He scanned my body. "Judging by your lack of jewelry, I see you're not the flossing type."

I shook my head no.

"It's all good. Nothing wrong with that... Come let me introduce you to your fellow Dons," he said while leading the way back down the driveway towards the waiting group, who was all studying me and Jay closely. "They might be a little iffy. They not used to out-of-towners," he whispered back before we made it to them.

I locked eyes with each of them individually. Two men and one woman. All three were nicely dressed and covered in diamonds. Swagg wasn't playing about their love for flossing.

"You know I got to put the ladies first. This lovely lady right here is Sasha. She'll pimp a hoe or nigga better than Iceberg Slim himself. She owns a few strip clubs out here where she conducts most of her business," Swagg informed while motioning towards a petite Sasha. She had a head full of super-neat and long, golden dreads that almost matched her skin tone, and her honey hazel eyes intensified everything else about her. It was safe to say that she was gorgeous.

Sasha waved her hand like an England princess.

"This old head right here is Tadoe. He has been scamming since George Bush was in office. He runs a small camp, but they also my most profitable camp. I guess numbers don't matter, huh?" The question was rhetorical, so no one answered.

Tadoe was an older looking man with salt-and-pepper hair on his head and beard. He looked to be probably in his mid-forties. He was black like Jay and had an arrogance about himself that floated in the air. I could feel it as he nodded his head with his nose turned up slightly.

"Last, but definitely not least... This young demon right here is Venom. He's the enforcement around here. Got a camp full of young wolves trying to be just like him and trust me when I tell you... that's not a good thing," Swagg informed with much seriousness put into that last sentence.

"Wassup?" Venom said in a soft, smooth, voice that didn't match his exterior.

Swagg did right by calling him a demon because the nigga was a scary sight. He didn't have a disfigurement or anything, he just was a frightening looking dude. His dark grey eyes seemed to look past you, making it hard to keep eye contact. His sharp facial features added to his macho appearance. Even without an intro-duction from Swagg, I would've known to be cautious around him.

"Wassup y'all?" I responded with a cool nod of my head.

Swag motioned towards me. "This is Rondo. The young nigga from ATL that I was telling y'all about. Trapper of the year where he's from. Literally. Lil' nigga ran up a mill' ticket in less than four months. He was a Mobster four months ago, and now he's a made-man today. It's safe to say he's a living legend. And y'all better get used to this youngin' by his side. That's his cousin, and personal bodyguard, Jay. He's only eighteen with a track record that'll make Venom proud."

"Why they bring you all the way out here from the A?" asked Sasha. "I asked this nigga, Swagg, but he just told me to ask you, soooooo..."

I looked Sasha up-and-down. I couldn't deny her prettiness, but she didn't have enough hips for me, so I hope she wasn't flirting. "Camp wasn't big enough for me and my Don. Instead of getting me whacked, he found me my own camp," I answered honestly. There was no point in lying.

"You know that nigga DG Ronte?" Venom asked.

I nodded my head. "Hell yeah. That's the lil' bro. We were in the same camp before he blew up. We weren't best friends or nothin' like that, but I definitely know him. I ran into him about a month ago. I got a picture with me and him on my Instagram page."

"That's wassup! I got to follow you on there, bruh," Venom responded enthusiastically.

Swagg nodded his knuckle shaped head in approval. "Glad to see y'all two getting along because guns and drugs go hand-in-hand, so y'all gon' need a close relationship. You don't have to deal with Tadoe or Sasha like that though. Their camps are independent. I'm a traveling man, so you won't see too much of me for real. The city is y'alls to run," he finished before hopping in the back of his Rolls Royce truck.

As Swagg's driver cruised off, Tadoe walked off towards his house on the other end of the neighborhood without another word.

"What's his problem?" I asked after he was out of hearing range.

Sasha waved her hand dismissively. "Oh, don't worry about him. He's just one of those niggas who's been getting money forever and thinks he's better than everybody. He and his whole camp. They all think they some Gods, or something."

I shrugged my shoulders. "Is what it is."

"Good response. Well, I'm about to go get back to my husband. He acts like he's about to die if I'm gone for too long. I'll see you around youngin'. I'm two houses down where the pink Ferrari's parked," she informed before walking off as well.

Venom walked up closer. He was a little taller than me. "Swagg was right. Guns and drugs do well together. Redd and I did a lot of business because he's an evil nigga and wanted a lot of people dead. I don't get that feeling from you, but we still gon' have to be close because our camps need each other."

"You right," I agreed.

"I'm right next door to you. Go inside and get yourself together. I'll come over a lil' later on this afternoon to give you a tour of the city," Venom informed before walking off, but not before shaking me and Jay's hand.

"I fuck with that nigga," Jay informed after he was gone.

I snapped my head over at him and looked at him crazily. It was *very* rare that he liked anybody. He wasn't a people's person at all, so for him to say that was startling. However, it was a good thing, so I wouldn't say anything about it. "Let's go see what this house looking like."

Chapter 7

As soon as we walked in the house, I almost tripped over a pile of money and an iced-out DG chain sitting on top. "What the fuck?"

I picked up the small yellow sticky note that was stuck on the pendant of the chain and read it.

You a made-man now! This comes with the house right here. Welcome to Fayetteville!

Underboss Swagg

The money added up to exactly $144,000, and the chain was a choker with a two-inch DG pendant that was flooded with diamonds. I tried to give it to Jay, but he firmly refused. He said he didn't deserve it and told me to keep it.

The house had four bedrooms, five bathrooms, and a basement that I planned on turning into a man cave for me and Jay. The backyard was spacious and sectioned off from the rest, so I'd figure out what to do with that space sooner or later.

We were munching on some Domino's pizza I had ordered around 10:30 when the movers showed up with the first wave of furniture I had ordered. Nothing too major, just two beds and a nice set for the living room. I still had to order the rest. I wanted to get a feel for the house before filling it with furniture and decorating it.

I saw the movers out of the house and blessed them with a generous tip for their speedy services. I made my way back to the living room where Jay was sitting on the new white leather sofa firing up a blunt of that exotic weed that he loved so much.

I plopped down next to him with a huff. "Let me hit that shit a few times."

He looked at me exactly how I looked at him earlier, when he told me he fucked with Venom. "Say what?"

"Nigga, you heard me."

"You ain't been smoking for the past four months. What makes you want to start back now? I thought you were done," he asked.

I nodded my head in agreement. "Yeah, I was done. I promised my mama I'd leave that shit alone until I made it big. I think it's safe to say that I made it by now."

Jay thought about it for a second before shrugging his shoulders. "Yeah, you right... Fuck it. Here you go."

I grabbed the blunt from him and took four deep pulls from it. As the potent smoke filled my lungs, I had no choice but to release a series of coughs. "That's that gas right there!" I complimented before passing the blunt back.

I started bobbing my head to the music Jay played from his phone as the high kicked in. Four months sober was enough to bring Wiz Khalifa's tolerance for weed to an all-time low, so you could only imagine how I felt. I was higher than a giraffe's pussy already.

I was a pothead for as long as I could remember, and I loved the feeling that Mary Jane brought me, but the feeling was way different now. The high hit way different now that I was a made-man. Life was good. I couldn't explain the feeling. I felt accomplished and secure. Two of the best feelings in life.

Jay tried to pass it back, but I waved him off. I knew my limits. I was high enough and wanted to be functional for our ride through the city.

***

Venom pulled up around two in his pitch-black 2014 AMG Mercedes Benz. He was the tour guide, so it made sense for him to drive. I sat up front with him and Jay hopped in the back.

Venom drove us around the city. He showed us the mall, where the good restaurants, shooting range, clubs were all located.

He took us everywhere where people went for entertainment. Like any other city, Fayetteville consisted of four sides. He informed us that the city was split up in two. The south and the east side was Dilluminati territory, and the west and north side belonged to the Crips. There were small cliques here and there, but Dilluminati and the Crips ruled.

We were crushing up Bragg Boulevard on the way to Shaw Road on the south side. Venom fired up a blunt and passed it over to me. I took four decent pulls and passed it back to Jay.

Venom was giving it to me straight about how Dilluminati rocked in their city, and I respected him for it. "Now, I can see already that you a smooth laid-back type of nigga, and that's cool, but these niggas out here used to Redd's aggressiveness. It'll be easy for them to take yo' coolness for weakness. I'm not telling you to step out of yo' character or nothing like that, but you definitely gon' have to be firm with these niggas. Ain't nothing but some wolves, snakes, and vultures out here, so you gon' have to make 'em respect you."

I nodded my head but remained silent. I was digesting the information and mentally preparing myself for the colossal task ahead of me.

Jay, on the other hand, had something to say about that. "Oh, examples gon' be made if they even think about trying that one. I can promise you that," he informed matter-a-factly after passing the blunt back to Venom.

Venom chuckled while shaking his head from side-to-side. "I got no doubt that you gon' handle business, lil' nigga, and I understand yo' job to protect Rondo, but the truth is that he's gonna have to make them respect *him*. If niggas only respect you, they'll find a way to get you out the way just to weaken him. They can't do shit to him cause he a made-man. I don't know how it is where y'all from, but a nigga gotta earn his respect around here, made-men and all."

"I definitely appreciate you for keeping it a hundred with a nigga like that. It's gon' go a long way with me, but to be honest, I was planning on being firm with these niggas anyway. As far as respect goes, I don't want it no other way but the hard way. I'm a young nigga, only twenty-four, and I'm not from around here, so I'm at a disadvantage. But I beat the odds before, and plan on doing it again," I boasted confidently.

"That's the attitude you gon' need to survive this shit, and it doesn't make it no better that you got the biggest camp in the city." He tried to pass me the blunt back, but I declined.

I nodded with my lips pursed. "I don't know if that's a good or bad thing yet, but time gon' definitely tell."

***

We pulled up to Ridge Park. It was a big ass trailer park off of Shaw Road, and the sight of it threw me for a loop. The only time I'd seen one was in the movie *8 Mile*, I'd never seen one in real life.

"We got apartment complexes too, but the trailer parks count as the hood too. It be going down out here," Venom informed. He must've read my mind.

I nodded my understanding.

"Oh yeah, one more thing. These folks out here throw barbeques and parties a lot, but this celebration right here is for you. They not gon' admit it, but just know it's for you," he informed seriously while parking in a line of other cars.

The trailer park was on a hill. From the looks of it, it was set up like a maze. When we got towards the bottom where the barbeque was taking place, I realized that it was a one way in and one way out type of community. Something that could definitely be used to their advantage.

There were a lot of people out enjoying the good food and loud music. The temperature had crept up to a chilly 55 degrees, but they didn't seem to care about the weather at all. Niggas, females, and kids were out kicking it. And to think that this gathering was for me, felt good. Nevertheless, I didn't get a big head.

When we hopped out of the car, it's like all eyes were on us. Everyone was curious about their new Don. A group of four niggas and a female walked up to us.

"This is Don Rondo and his shooter, DG Jay," Venom introduced us to them. "Rondo, these are your Mafiosos right here. I'm about to go grab me some of this food while y'all get acquainted and shit."

"I heard you be fuckin' with DG Ronte," one of them stated with much interest.

"Yeah, I do... Who supposed to be the top Mafioso?" I asked with a straight face. I didn't mean to brush their question off, but this wasn't time for gossip. I had to show them I was about business off the top.

A bright skinned dread-head spoke up, "Right here. They call me DG Trappa."

"Okay cool. I'm definitely gon' chop it up with the rest of y'all, but I need to holla at this nigga Trappa first." I wasn't aggressive, but I was firm. It fit me well because I actually did mean business, and I didn't come to play.

The rest of the Mafiosos nodded before walking away. I didn't sense any resentment or anything. It's like they understood, and that was a good start. I started walking at a snail's pace and Trappa fell in line beside me while Jay brought up the rear. "How many Mobsters on count for our camp?"

He hesitated. "Umm, between a hundred thirty and a hundred forty. Some shit like that."

"How much money we pulling in as a whole?" I asked while glancing at different people who were staring at us.

"I don't know, to tell you the truth, but we definitely getting to the money. Redd never gave a fuck what we made, or how we made it, as long as we paid our dues to him on time," he answered truthfully, and I knew it was the truth so I couldn't fault him.

"Well, I'm gon' let you know this right now. I'm not Redd. I care how much money y'all make and how y'all make it. We gon' enjoy this here get together right now, but I'm gon' need you and the rest of the Mafiosos to be up early in the morning because I'm holding a meeting at my house at 8:00 sharp. No exceptions. By the looks of it, we got a lot of work to do."

Trappa nodded his understanding. "Your word is law, Don. Matter-a-fact, I'm about to go tell them right now... That is if I'm dismissed."

"Go ahead," I instructed as if another man asking me for permission to be excused didn't faze me. This made-man shit would definitely take some getting used to.

Jay walked up to my side as Trappa walked away towards the rest of the Mafiosos, who were speaking in a group amongst themselves. "This gon' be one helluva journey."

"Why you say that? What you thinking?" I asked while looked over at him.

"I'm thinking we don't belong out here, but we don't got a choice, so we just gon' have to make the best out of this shit."

I nodded my head in agreement. "Let's go see what this food talking about. That weed got me hungry as fuck."

Chapter 8

After we left from the barbeque, it was about eight o'clock, and the sun had just about disappeared for the night. The temperature was dropping, so the gathering got cut short. I enjoyed the food and the company of the Mobsters in my camp. I was sure that they just wanted to play under me because I was the Don and I knew one of the hottest rappers in the game, but that was to be expected. I planned on using it to my advantage.

Apparently, the barbeque wasn't the end of the tour. We ended up at a strip club called *Sparkles*. I already knew that Sasha owned every strip club in the area, so I wasn't surprised when she met us at the door.

"I'm glad y'all came through," she informed brightly. "I see now you got a helluva swag on you, boy. Where you get that pea coat from?" she asked me while scanning me up and down approvingly.

"I ordered this online. It's that Alexander McQueen muthafucka," I informed while looking down at my icy white attire.

"Okay. I see you! Come on in y'all. It's early, but y'all still gon' have some fun."

The club was nice. Nothing over-the-top, but definitely far from a hole-in-the-wall. I'd been through my strip club phase when I was twenty-one, so I'd seen my share of strip clubs. However, to compare this with the experience I had in Atlanta wouldn't be fair. It wasn't an Atlanta strip club, but it was good for Fayetteville.

Attractive women sashayed around the place confidently seducing the mild crowd of customers who came to enjoy themselves. The place had a little size on it too. There were two big stages, and a big round bar in the middle of the spot.

Sasha led us to the best VIP booth in the building. It was the only one that required stairs to enter. "Usually, I be in my office doing paperwork and watching the floor through my monitors, but since this your first day out in the Ville, I'm gon' show you a nice time personally."

"I appreciate that. You got some nice girls working up in here though," I complimented while scanning the floor from the balcony while leaning on the rail. She ran a nice little operation, and the fact that it was legal on the surface made it that much better.

"What kind of woman do you prefer? I got all kinds of bitches in here, and if I don't have them at this club, I can order them from another."

It didn't take long for me to answer. "I guess I'm a traditional dope boy because I like mines pretty in the face, small in the waist, and big in the ass."

"Say less. Got plenty of that in here," she said with a chuckle.

She walked off, and I went to sit on the couch with Venom and Jay, who were being entertained by the two strippers that were already in the VIP booth when we came.

I was bobbing my head to the music and puffing on a blunt of weed when Sasha came back with a line of half-naked bitches. Three of them were Black, and one was Hispanic. They all lined up in front of the couch.

"Go ahead and pick."

I scanned the females carefully. I settled on a redhead and the Hispanic. Both were pretty and curvy just how I liked them. The rest walked away while the selected ones remained standing like two stallions.

"Usually, I would've charged you $1,000 to take both of them for a spin, but like I said, this night of fun is on me, so have fun," she said with a bright smile before handing me two Magnum condoms.

I grabbed the condoms. "Damn, that's wassup. I thought you was telling me to pick them for a lap dance or some shit."

"They gon' give you all that and some." Sasha stood up, walked over to the two girls, and had a brief talk with them before walking off.

The red-headed Black girl walked up to me and extended her hand for me to grab. I grabbed it and she led me out of the booth with the Hispanic bringing up the rear. Jay tried to come with me, but I told him that I was good and to enjoy himself.

There were a series of exotic back rooms reserved for private dances. They led me into one of them and pushed me down onto the soft leather sofa. The rooms had to be soundproof because there was a different set of music playing inside and I couldn't even hear the music that was blasting on the floor. We'd entered our own world.

The sexy tattooed Hispanic woman brought me a touchscreen tablet that was nearly identical to an iPad mini. There were two options to choose from lights and music. I clicked on the music, and a long playlist of club bangers popped up. Future's *Turn on the Lights* was playing and I liked that song, so I let it ride. I went back and hit the other option. The lights were already red and they had several color options on the tablet, but I pressed shuffle. The lights went from red, yellow, blue, and purple, in a repeated motion.

I felt like I was in a rap video as I watched them get sexy on the stage. The redhead had climbed high on the pole doing a spin on her way down with her legs spread eagle, and the Hispanic was on all fours twerking her ass making the tattooed butterfly on her ass soar.

It's been almost two weeks since I had my dick wet. Ever since I hopped on my road to riches, I'd been so focused that I had to make appointments to get my rocks off. Now that I was a made-man, I could enjoy myself a little more. I'd done what my mother wanted already, so I felt comfortable lollygagging a little. I had room for it now.

I placed the tablet on the floor and got real comfortable on the couch as I watched the wonderful show. I took my skull cap off and removed my pea coat. My temperature, and my dick, was rising at the same rate.

The Hispanic wore a cute bikini, and the redhead was draped in a see-through catsuit. Me rubbing my erection through my jeans must've been a signal for them because they quickly made their way over to the couch before helping me remove the rest of my clothes. When it was all said and done, I was sitting there with nothing but a chain on my neck and a pair of white Gucci socks on my feet.

There was nothing to talk about, so they both filled their mouths with a piece of me. The Hispanic deep throated my dick, while the redhead popped both of my balls in her mouth and sucked on them like they were coated with milk chocolate. I leaned back on the sofa with my eyes closed while gripping a handful of the Hispanic's silky hair.

At that moment, my mind was clear. I had tunnel vision. The only thing I cared about was catching a nut. I made myself cum quick. The Hispanic woman looked up at me in surprise after I filled her mouth with cum, but I told her to keep sucking and I eventually bricked up again. I just had to get that first one out the way so I could perform properly. I played it cool, but this was my first threesome with two women and I wanted to make the most out of it.

I motioned for them to stop before standing up and telling them to get on the couch. After quickly removing their clothes, they both put their knees on the couch with their asses poking out. I slid one of the condoms on and wasted no time. The red head's pussy looked better from behind, so I tried her out first. I gripped her weave as I pumped away.

The Hispanic got up and started rubbing on my chest, not wanting to feel left out, so I started sucking on her pierced nipples without losing my stride. After I'd had enough of that position, I made them both get on the floor. The redhead laid on her back with her legs spread, and the Hispanic woman got on her knees with her ass in the air and her face in the red head's pussy.

I slid into the Hispanic woman from behind and got excited. Unlike the redhead, her shit was tight and gripped my dick pleasantly. I started hitting her with the slow and deep stroke while slapping her big ass every now-and-then. I even popped a thumb in her ass while she threw it back on the dick.

I couldn't help myself, after two minutes, I was out the door. I snatched the condom off and nutted on her ass. The redhead got up and started licking the cement up off of her ass. I just smirked looking down at their freaky asses.

I made one of them go get some weed for us to smoke while we took a break. I planned on using the other condom before it was all over with.

Malik D. Rice

Chapter 9

I didn't get much sleep that night. I partied hard and the weed had me wanting to stay in bed, but I had shit to do. Sleep could wait. I let Jay get his sleep while I took a trip to the grocery store to pick up a few things for the spot so we wouldn't have to keep ordering out every time we got hungry.

When I pulled back up to the house, I saw two Escalades parked in the wraparound driveway with the Mafiosos standing outside of them talking amongst themselves. I'm glad they all made it on time because I would've hated to have to make an example out of one of them so early.

I drove past them and parked in my driveway. I attempted to get my grocery bags out the back, but Trappa refused and made two of the other Mafiosos grab them. I told them to sit in the living room while I put the groceries away.

After that, I walked into the living room and joined them. "Swagg gave me a nice amount of money for coming out here and taking Redd's place. I'm gon' give that to one of y'all to flip, and I'm gon' use the profit to pay my dues to him from here on out. What I'm gon' do is give another one of y'all a nice amount of money to flip, so y'all can use the profit from that to pay me my dues. That way y'all can use the original dues to put back into the camp for the betterment."

Every last one of them looked surprised by what I said, but neither of them said a word, so I continued. "Like I told Trappa yesterday, I'm not Redd. I see that he left me a mess to clean up. I know y'all used to rockin' a certain way, but those times are up. Dilluminati's not a gang, it's an organization, and organizations are organized. I'm not gon' talk y'all heads off though because I'm gon' definitely show y'all better than I can tell."

"That's some real shit right there... You finished?" Trappa asked.

"For now," I answered before grabbing the money that I got from Swagg and gave it to Trappa. I made sure to tell him exactly what to bring back, and that he was responsible for the dues I had to pay Swagg.

After that, I scanned the group of Mafiosos and randomly picked one of them to stay behind. His name was DG Tory. He was twenty-eight with a body full of tattoos and a lazy eye.

I planned on spending a little time with each of them one-on-one. It would make the learning process easier for me. Get to see where all of their heads were at individually. Mafiosos are the backbone to any camp, so I had to make sure the ones up under me belonged.

***

An hour later, I was pulling up into a ground-level apartment complex just off of Bragg Boulevard. This was Tory's domain. Every Mafioso had their own section to rule over. It gave the organization more ground to cover. We did the same thing back in Atlanta, and I was glad that they at least had that much structure in place.

There were a few people out hugging the block despite the cold weather. "This my hood right here. I got twenty-four niggas up under me of all ages. Don't nothing but weed, pills, and crack sell over here," Tory informed from the passenger's seat while scanning the block like a proud CEO.

We stepped out of the car and walked up the walkway to his apartment. Before he could put his key into the door, a cute chubby woman with a Burberry scarf wrapped around her head snatched the door open. "Where the fuck you been nigga? I wake up and yo' ass is long gone," she asked before looking me up-and-down unimpressively, "And who the fuck is this nigga here?"

"This is Don Rondo and his cousin, Jay... I was gone this morning because he called a meeting for all the Mafiosos." Tory informed matter-a-factly.

I watched the sassy look instantly evaporate from her face. It was replaced by a startled expression. "Oh my Godddd! I'm soooo sorry, sir! I didn't know you were Don Rondo. Please forgive me. Come on in. Can I get you anything?" Seeing her whole attitude switch up at the mention of my title showed me firsthand how easy it was for made-men in Dilluminati to be so prideful, but I promised to remain as humble as possible. No matter how much praise I received.

We stepped into the apartment. Jay and I took a seat on the bigger couch while Tory went to the back. "You got some Kool-Aid?" I asked.

"I'll make some for you right now. Y'all gon' stay for breakfast, right? I was going to order something, but since you're here, I'll make something nice," she asked.

Since Jay hadn't eaten yet and the weed that I smoked earlier had me hungry again, I told her to go ahead. When she disappeared into the kitchen, Tory reappeared in the living room with a spiral notepad in his hand.

He handed me the notepad before taking a seat on the smaller couch. "Trappa made everybody make them lists yesterday. Never told us what to do with them, just that you wanted them made, so there you go."

I looked over the list carefully. It was a list of all of the Mobsters under his command. Their names, birthdays, and positions. "Good, now I'm gon' need you to collect the lists from the other Mafiosos because you're going to keep track of the count in this camp. If anybody recruits a new Mobster, they need to end up on your list."

Tory looked at me unenthusiastically. "Does it have to be me?"

"I mean, I chose you for it. So yeah, it has to be you."

I could tell that Tory wasn't happy with the task, but he didn't argue. I spent the rest of the morning questioning him about things that I was curious about over the big breakfast his baby mother had cooked. After his five-year-old daughter did a series of dances for everybody, Jay and I hit the road.

Chapter 10

Cross Creek Mall was the biggest mall in the city of Fayetteville. There were a few strip malls in the area and a few big malls in the surrounding cities, but this was the only big mall inside of the city. When we came yesterday with Venom, we only took a brief stroll through. I didn't get a chance to look around like I wanted to, so I came back. Now, I could look around and shop how I wanted.

It was Sunday, so the mall wasn't packed like it was yesterday, but it was definitely far from empty. Fayetteville wasn't as small of a city as I was thinking. There were definitely lots of people out here.

We went store-to-store checking out different things. The majority of my new wardrobe consisted of high-end designers, so I was picking up regular name brands that I also favored. Jay and I had to go drop our clothes off in the car before going back inside for the shoes because we knew we were about to go overboard.

There were about four other customers in Footlocker when we walked inside. I noticed right away that they were Dilluminati by their tattoos. I couldn't help but notice two of them at the checkout counter giving this Caucasian man a hard time as he tried to assist them. I could tell the man was getting fed up with their shenanigans and probably was too scared to speak up for himself, but that didn't make it right.

They were so focused on harassing the man that they hadn't seen us enter the store. "Fours up!" I greeted sharply, startling them.

"A-all the time... Who is you?" one of them asked after returning the greeting.

Another one of them pointed at me with wide eyes. "That's Don Rondo, nigga! Where you was at yesterday?" he asked the one who spoke first.

"Exactly. I take it y'all in my camp?" I asked while glaring at each of them closely.

They all nodded in unison.

"I don't know about that right there. Y'all can't be in my camp out here oppressing civilians making me look bad. I might need to transfer y'all over to Venom's camp. Sound like something his Mobster's get into."

Now they all shook their heads from side-to-side in unison. Venom only had twenty Mobsters in his camp for a reason. A lot of niggas weren't cut out for their lifestyle.

"Alright then... Y'all done in here?" I asked.

"Yeah. We was just about to leave," one of them informed before they all quickly left the store.

"My bad, man. They're just young as hell and don't know no better." The youngins represented the same thing as me and they were my responsibility, so I felt obligated to apologize for their behavior.

The Caucasian man waved it off. "It's alright. I'll be fine... Just let me know when you're ready so I can assist you."

"No, it's alright, Jerry. I'll help them out. When you're ready just let me know. My name is Malika," a pretty little brown-skinned woman said from behind the counter.

She was sitting down, so I really didn't pay too much attention to her before because I was focused on the situation. Now that she was talking and standing, the spotlight was on her. I locked eyes with her briefly before walking off.

"You like her, huh?" Jay asked while nudging me with his sharp elbow playfully.

I looked at him with a smile I tried to suppress. "Shawty, you don't let shit get past you."

We both picked out a handful of sneakers each. Malika had to write down the specific shoe types with the sizes we needed. After we tried on all the shoes and paid for them at the cash register, we headed out.

Malika was being extra nice and friendly. She told me how much she admired what I did with my Mobsters and all, but I just played it cool. I was walking out of the store, but stopped dead in my tracks when I heard my mother's voice in my head.

"After you run up a check and get where you need to be in life, that's when you need to start really enjoying life. Don't lose your focus though. You still need to handle business. However, make time for yourself still. Get you a decent woman in your life... Have some kids. Have a lot of them, so our bloodline can live on. Your legacy will live on."

"Ma, you forgot about Chyanne?" I asked confusingly.

My mother rolled her eyes. "No, I ain't forget about your lil' girlfriend. Her true colors gon' show sooner or later. Once they do, you need to kick her ass straight to the curb and focus on your grind. Once you make it where you need to be, you need to snatch you up something decent."

I snapped back to reality and looked over at, Jay, who was looking at me in confusion. "You a'ight?" he asked with a raised brow.

"Yeah, hold on." I sat my bags down by his feet and walked back towards the cash register.

I locked eyes with, Malika, who was looking up at me expectantly from behind the counter. "You forgot something?" she asked as I approached.

"Yeah, your number."

Malik D. Rice

Chapter 11

The next morning, I spent an hour on a video conference with my new lawyer. He was one of the most efficient criminal defense attorneys in the state of North Carolina. Even though I didn't have plans on getting my hands dirty, shit still happened, so I was prepared. He was now on retainer for any legal issues that I might come across in the future.

Trappa texted me during my video conference, but the lawyer had my undivided attention, so I didn't check it until afterwards. He said he needed to meet with me as soon as possible, so I told him to pull up to the house.

He must've been on the road already because it didn't take long for him to pull up. I threw on a Moncler jacket and walked outside to meet him. I hopped in the back of the Escalade with him. The Mobster that he had behind the wheel got out so we could converse privately.

"Talk to me," I said after the driver's door shut.

He didn't say a word. He reached between his legs and came up with a small gym bag. He handed it over to me.

"What's this for?" I asked after looking inside the bag at all the hundreds.

"The owners of seven different businesses in the area paid their monthly payment. Usually, Redd would go around and collect all his dues personally. Of course, Redd never showed up, so they called my phone. I picked it all up, but Redd's gone, so I guess that belongs to you."

I scratched my head with a confused expression etched on my face. "Wait. That don't make no sense. Why Redd got businesses on our payroll? He a dope boy, that's what Venom's supposed to be doing."

Trappa shook his head causing his black-and-blonde dreads to shake with it. "Nah, man. Venom takes hits and sends his Mobsters out of town on heists. That's how he makes his money. Let him tell it, ain't no money in extortion, so he don't even bother... Redd, being the nigga that he is, had to get a piece of it, so he started pushing up on business owners and shit."

I shook my head disappointedly. "How long this been going on?"

"Since before Dilluminati even hit Fayetteville," Trappa answered matter-a-factly.

I fished my phone from my pocket and called Jay telling him to come outside and lock the door behind him. Once Jay was in the truck, I told Trappa to call the first business owner and to set a meeting up with them.

About thirty minutes later, we were in the parking lot of a Red Lobster restaurant near the mall. A dark red Mercedes Benz coupe pulled up next to the truck.

"That's him right there," Trappa informed with a nod.

The owner's name was Mark Timothy. He was an old, heavyweight, Italian man. He tried to get out of the car, but I told him to get back in as I walked around the hood to the passenger's side. Once inside the car, I tossed a small stack of money onto his lap.

"What's this for?" he asked hesitantly. Fear was sliding off him like the sweat on his face.

"My name is Rondo, and I'm taking over for Redd. I'm aware of the arrangement you had with him, but I'm here to let you know that it's terminated. I'm not in the business of extortion, but I am a businessman. Instead of you paying me for protection, I'm going to pay you for a percentage of your business. We'll work out the details soon, I just wanted to return your money."

I ignored his shocked expression and got out of the car. There was no time for reassurance. I had to meet with six more business owners and have the same conversation.

I spent a few hours on FaceTime with Malika last night, and I'd been texting her throughout the day. She was younger than the females I usually dealt with, but I liked the way she carried herself. I never would've known she was twenty unless she told me. I thought she was my age.

She'd been out of high school for a couple of years. She worked at Footlocker even though her mother was a doctor at the local hospital and her father was a retired NFL player.

When she broke the news about her father on FaceTime, I raised an eyebrow. She gave me his name and told me to look him up. He'd spent his whole twelve-year career playing for the Cincinnati Bengals as a second-string corner-back. As soon as she gave me his name, I knew who she was talking about because I was big on football.

She told me that he never stayed with her and her mother, but he sent money steadily and even had a healthy trust fund set up for her when she turned twenty-one. She just got the job at Footlocker so she could appreciate the value of hard-earned money. She planned on investing in her own shoe line after she turned twenty-one.

I told her about my mother's death, Chyanne's deceit, and the reason behind me moving to Fayetteville. I knew I really wasn't supposed to be opening up to her like that and trusting her with that information, but it was something about her. She seemed so trustworthy and made a nigga feel comfortable when talking to her.

By the time I was done meeting all the businessmen, It was about six o'clock. Malika wanted to cook me dinner and bond face-to-face. Her mother was at work and her little brother was at his friend's house. I didn't have anything but snacks in the house and it's been a while since I had a home-cooked meal, so after Trappa dropped us off, we hopped in my car and followed the GPS to her house.

"Damn! You sure we going to meet the same girl that worked in Footlocker?" Jay asked while looking around at all the magazine-ready houses in the suburban neighborhood.

I nodded my head. "Yeah, that's her. I would've never known... At least I don't have to worry about her gold-digging a nigga for his money," I joked seriously.

She stayed in a beautiful mini-mansion that resembled mines, but was a little bigger. I parked my car next to a purple Jaguar in the driveway.

"Damn, you got to reel shawty in. She got to come from some type of money," said Jay as we got out of the car.

I told him about her father as we walked up the driveway to the front door. I could tell he had plenty of questions to ask, but they'd have to wait because Malika had opened the door and was waiting for us at the door.

She had on a pair of blue Robin jeans, a white True Religion halter top, and a pair of white Christian Louboutin on her feet. She didn't have a gigantic ass, but it was definitely enough for me to work with. "You lookin' good, shawty. I like them shoes."

"You're not the only one with red bottoms around here," she teased, referring to the shoes I wore in Footlocker when we met. "You don't look too bad yourself," she returned the compliment while looking me up-and-down approvingly.

I looked down at my attire. I had on a Ralph Lauren V-neck t-shirt up under my Moncler jacket and a pair of True Religion jeans. The only thing I wore that wasn't white were my wheat Timberland boots. It was something simple. I guess my chain and grill completed the whole dope boy look because she was literally looking at me with heart eyes. "I just threw something on. I've been ripping-and-running since this morning."

She nodded her head slowly. "I see you didn't forget to bring your bodyguard with you," she joked before letting us into the house.

"Damn, this spot nice. I need the same decorator y'all had because my shit still empty as hell," I stated.

"I can help you with that. I helped my mommy decorate in here after she had the whole place remodeled. You guys can chill in the living room, I'm halfway done with the meal."

Malika's mother taught her good when it came to cooking. She made steak with a shrimp salad on the side. It was so good that I made her fix me a second plate.

We were eating in the living room. Jay sat in the Lay-Z-Boy chair watching the movie on TV, while Malika and I sat on one of the sofas. I was focused on my food, and she was watching me. I felt her eyes burning into the side of my skull, but I ignored her for a second.

After a full minute passed, and I still felt her eyes on me, I finally said something. "Where I come from, staring is considered kind of rude."

"I'm sorry. I was just thinking," she informed.

I looked up from my plate. "This the part where I ask what you got on yo' mind?"

"Yes, it is, smart ass!" she spat while hitting me in the shoulder playfully. "But seriously... I was just thinking about how Christmas is coming up, and you literally don't have anyone to share it with. I couldn't imagine not having any family, but you, you're just so damn nonchalant. It's crazy."

I shrugged my shoulders. "In some ways, I feel like my mama is still with me, but other than that, it's just me and Jay. This the hand I was dealt, so it is what it is."

"I'll be here for you," she informed while gazing at me seriously.

"That's good to know, but I don't want no pity from you, shawty. If you gon' fuck with me, do it because you really fuck with me and not just because you feel sorry for me."

Chapter 12

I woke up at eleven the next morning, which was late for me. I believed in early starts, so I was kind of upset, but there was nothing I could do about it. I just grabbed the half-smoked blunt out of the ashtray on the nightstand and fired it up.

I enjoyed the little dinner date I had with Malika last night. She was a real lady with goals and plenty of respect for herself. I had to give her that, and the fact that Jay seemed to like her was definitely a plus.

I was a Pisces, and I loved to love just as much as I loved to be loved. The real definition of a lover boy, as my mother used to say, so it felt good to have a spark with a new female. But as much as I wanted to linger on Malika and our growing interest in each other, I still had an entire empire to clean up. Redd left a big mess for me to clean up, and I planned on doing just that.

When I was finished with my camp, they'd be thanking me. Right now, they couldn't see what I was trying to do, but over time, they would. I hopped up out of the bed full of motivation and headed into the bathroom ready to start my day.

***

"What the fuck going on out here?" I asked as we pulled up into another trailer park off of Shaw Road.

I was there to meet with Rod. He was the oldest Mafioso in my camp. I talked to him a few hours ago letting him know that I would be pulling up on him, and he told me it was all good. But by the looks of things, it wasn't all good.

He sat on the dirt ground with his back against an old school Chevy with his head tucked in his knees. There were two ladies sitting on the ground with him on either side, and a bigger group of spectators stood around them talking amongst themselves.

"I don't know, but something definitely done happened out here," Jay said while putting out his blunt in the ashtray and gripping his Glock23 out of precaution.

I parked the car on the concrete road that ran between the trailers and hopped out. All eyes were on us as we walked up on them. The closer I got, I noticed that there were a lot of teary eyes in the crowd.

"This a bad time?" I asked standing over Rod and the two women. One looked to be around his age, and the other was a lot younger.

Rod lifted his head slowly and looked up at me with one of the evilest looks I'd ever seen on a man's face in my entire life. "What the fuck you think?" His voice was deep and sharp.

Before I could say another word, the younger woman quickly stood up and ushered us away from Rod. She led us back to the street. "Please don't hold that against him. That's my daddy. My older brother just got gunned down by some police officers on the east side, so this a rough time right now. He's not in his right mind, that was his best friend."

"Damnnnn, shawty! I'm sorry to hear that. Tell that nigga to hit me if he needs anything. I'm sorry for y'all loss," I said before getting back into the car and driving off.

I felt bad that Rod was going through a crisis, but business is business and it has to continue at all cost, so I went down the list and pulled up on the next Mafioso.

Nequa was the only female Mafioso in my camp. I couldn't tell if she was a dike or not, but I knew she was a real hustler who'd earned her stripes as a Mafioso in my camp and that's all I needed to know. She had authority over a neighborhood right off of Bragg Boulevard. It consisted of a series of rundown houses. I could tell from first glance that it was a serious area.

She told me to meet her at the neighborhood store at the entrance of the hood on Bragg Boulevard. There were about six Mobsters posted on the side of the store, and I recognized one of them from Footlocker the other day. I didn't see Nequa, so I called her phone. She told me she was inside of the store.

As Jay and I were walking across the parking lot towards the store, one of the Monsters from the side of the store came jogging up to us. Jay swiftly stepped in front of me while shoving me to the other side.

"Nah, it ain't nothing like that bruh! I'm far from stupid. I just want a quick word with the Don real quick," he informed with both hands in the air.

I stepped forward. "What's going on?" I asked curiously. I wanted to hear what he had to say. He was the first Mobster that approached me since I'd been out here.

"Listen, I know you going in there to meet with Nequa, but I just need you to hear me out for a few minutes, *please*." The desperation in his eyes was severe. Whatever it was he wanted to address was clearly important to him.

I nodded my head for him to continue.

"Listen, I'm sixteen with four kids out here. This lil' money I'm makin' on the block barely enough to take care of the two that live with me, let alone the other two. Something got to give," he informed.

I was shocked at the news, but I didn't show it because I didn't want him to feel self-conscious. I felt responsible for him and his kids. "I understand yo' situation and I'm taking steps right now to set shit straight so everybody can eat how they're supposed to out here. I know shit fucked up right now, just give me a lil' time to get it right," I promised seriously.

He shook his head side-to-side. "Nah, bro. I'm trying to make it out. I know you cool with Ronte, so I just want you to listen to my shit."

"I don't know, lil' bro. I'm not in the music business."

"I'm telling you. I'm sick with this rap shit, big bro. Just listen to my shit. If you don't like it, I'll let you take my next week's pay," he challenged confidently.

I gave him a sideways look through squinted eyes. He had to be nice to say something like that. "Alright, go ahead. Let me hear something."

"Oh, I was just going to email you the songs, but I'll give you a live one if you want."

I nodded my head slightly. "Oh, that's even better." I took his phone and typed my email in before giving it back to him. "If I don't like that shit, you ain't getting paid next week," I warned as I walked off.

"It's a bet!" he shouted from behind.

I caught him doing a fist-pump in the reflection on the store's window and smiled brightly. I would definitely check his shit out as soon as I got the chance.

Nequa was in the back area of the store where they kept the slot machines. It was a small room that only held four machines. Three Mobsters stood guard in front of the room while she played.

I told Jay to post up with the Mobsters while I chopped it up with Nequa. She was tall for a woman. A little shorter than me and probably weighed about two-hundred pounds, but she was pretty in the face. Light-bright with dimples. She was a cutie, but I could tell she had a bad attitude. I felt it in her energy when I was around her.

"Looks like you having fun in here." I observed while taking a seat on the stool at the next machine over.

She shrugged her shoulders. "Not for real... I just come in here when I got a lot on my mind. For some reason, it helps."

"You better than me. When I got a lot on my mind, I go to talking to my dead mama," I informed jokingly, but the seriousness was still there.

She looked over at me slowly with agitation on her face. "Is it something specific you wanted to meet with me about?"

I was kind of startled by her cold response, but I understood. Even though I was her new Don, she still didn't know me, and probably didn't trust me either. "Don't worry about it. I'm not a friendly person either. This extra communication shit is new to me, but yeah, it is a reason I wanted to meet with you. I'm gon' put you in charge of the loans for the whole camp."

"Loans? That shit new to me," she asked in confusion.

"Yeah, loans... I'm gon' get you some work to flip and you gon' start the loan pot with that. That way if somebody needs a loan, they can just get it from the camp. That goes for Mobsters and civilians that stay on our territories. So, if somebody wants a loan for something, they can just come to us instead of going to the bank. Plus, that's another way to get the community on our side instead of having them secretly hating us."

She stared at me with interest for a few seconds. "Damn! I can't even lie, that's a good ass idea bruh. It's a less chance that an old couple would call the police on the Mobsters if Dilluminati is helping pay their bills and putting food on their table."

I placed a hand on her shoulder and looked her dead in the eyes. "Exactly... I'm not here to flex my muscle and make everybody bow down to me, shawty. I'm trying to lift this shit up... I'm trying to lift y'all up," I assured before standing up and walking out of the room.

Malik D. Rice

Chapter 13

I gave Malika the address to my house, and she pulled up. She only worked part-time, so she had a lot of free time. Free time that she was now investing in me. Seems like I wasn't the only one intrigued. She admitted that she felt more alive when she was in my presence, and it didn't have anything to do with the fact that I was the first real street nigga that she ever fucked with.

When she pulled up, the cable man was connecting cable to the three TV's that I had ordered. One for the living room, and the other two for me and Jay's room.

"Oh my Godddd! Why'd you downplay your house like this? It's beautiful, and the location is perfect! I can only imagine what you paid for it," she said while looking around in amazement.

"I ain't paid shit. You know how some people got company cars? Well, this is a company house," I joked seriously.

She smiled. "One helluva company I see."

"Everything got its ups and downs."

After the cable was installed, Jay retired to his room so Malika and I could enjoy a little privacy. I'd already told him that she made it known off the top that it would be a minute before we had sex, but he still wanted to give us our space, and I understood.

We were watching a movie on demand when I thought about the bet I'd made earlier with the youngin at the store. I paused the movie suddenly.

"Hey! That movie was getting good." She pouted with her lip poked out playfully.

I assured her that I would go back to the movie after I played a few of the songs. I went onto my email and played three of his songs on my phone. His name was DG Manny.

"Damn! That's really nice. I like that," she admitted while bopping her head to the rhythm of the music.

I was doing the same. I couldn't lie, the young nigga had real talent. Before I knew it, we went through the whole sixteen songs and I couldn't honestly say that there was only one that I didn't like. That was rare.

Malika asked me to email the songs to her so she could listen to them on her own time. After that, I told her all about the bet I had with Manny and what I now planned on doing for him.

"It's so cool how you know a world-famous rapper personally. Must be nice," she said referring to Ronte.

I waved her off nonchalantly. "I mean, me and Ronte definitely from the same hood and whatnot, but we ain't friends for real. He just a lil' nigga from the hood that I used to see around. After he got famous, he never paid me any attention until I started getting money for real."

"Well, you still know him, and he shouted you out on his Instagram page. That's *way* more than a lot of people could say. Andddd you have the power to give that young dude, Manny, a real shot to get out of the hood and be there for all his kids," she philosophized with a hand on my knee for effect.

I took a deep breath and thought deep on what she'd just said. "You're right. I like that about you though, shawty. It's like every time I even try to think negative, you say some ol' positive ass shit that flips my whole mindset."

"It's a challenge to look at the bright side of things, but it's definitely not impossible, so I just try my hardest," she informed humbly.

I looked at her and smiled slightly. She just didn't know how much I needed her affection at the moment. The fact that she was passionate like me was a big plus.

"Whatttttt?" she asked shyly with a blush. Her smile was contagious, and her personality matched her beauty.

"All this shit... My whole life, even you, been feeling like a dream lately. Kind of hard to explain the feeling." I knew the genuineness in my eyes, and voice reached her as she stared back at me all dreamlike.

"You probably won't believe me when I tell you this because of the speed that we're going, but the honest truth is that I'm not a big fan of rushed relationships or men that are into the streets, but it's just..." She stared off. I guess she was trying to find the right words. "It's just right, I guess... Something about you draws me towards you, and the strength of it is amazing. It's not even just your appearance or the excitement of being with a man like you. You're different than the average street dude. Your intelligence and lack of ignorance intrigues me the most."

I leaned in and kissed her soft and glossy lips. It was something short, but sexy. I put my arm around her and pulled her in closely before cutting the movie back on. It was understood that we both were exactly where we needed to be.

Chapter 14

Late that same night, I met Trappa in Ridge Park. Jay was sleep and I didn't feel like waking him up, so I just hopped in my car and pulled up myself. From my understanding, security for made-men in Fayetteville was more of a precaution than an actual need. It's a small town, and everyone has an understanding for the most part, so unless there's a threat of war, there's no real need for security.

Ridge Park threw me for a loop once again as I sat there on a nice suede couch in Trappa's mobile home. Surprisingly, the inside of the trailer looked way better than the outside. I always thought it would be rugged, but I was wrong. Trappa had a nice little setup, but he wasn't where he needed to be, and that's why I was there. "Shawty, you definitely doing alright for yourself out here, but you could easily do way better."

"Look. I respect yo' position in Dilluminati and I'm impressed with yo' life story as a man, but I'm not gon' let you sit here and say that bruh. You wasn't there when my grandma got sick and I had to pick that seventy thousand dollars medical bill up. You wasn't there when I had to buy that house for my baby mama because I promised her that I wouldn't let my daughter grow up in the slums, and you damn sure wasn't there when two of my Mobster's died and I paid for both of their funerals out my own pockets," Trappa countered matter-a-factly.

I started to say something, but he cut me off. "Nah, just listen... I know I was supposed to be next up after Redd fell. I know Swagg didn't feel like I was ready for the Don position, and he was right. I'm not ready for that position yet, but I'm still not gon' let a nigga sit here and tell me that I'm not handling mines out here."

I sat up on the couch and looked over at him with apologetic eyes. "Listen, bro. I didn't mean to offend you, and that's not what I'm here for. I'm not trying to talk down on you or none of that lame ass shit. I'm just trying to motivate you, my nigga. I can already tell that it's a lot of potential out here and I'm just trying to make sure we prosper as a whole."

Knock! Knock! Knock!

"Yooo Trappa!" Someone was at the door and the urgency in their voice alerted me. I knew off the rip that something wasn't right.

Trappa sat his pit bull puppy down on the floor before getting up to answer the door. He left his pistol on the coffee table, so I resisted the urge to clutch on the one that sat in my lap.

"Why the hell you knockin' on my shit like you done lost yo' mind, Uno?" Trappa asked as he let a well-dressed heavy-set man into the spot.

"Bruh, you ain't gon' believe this shit right here!" Uno exclaimed. He was a yellow dude, who looked to be around my age, with an eye patch. It was clear where he got his name from.

Uno looked down at me and widened his good eye when he noticed who I was. "Oh, shit! Wassup Don? I didn't know you was up in here."

"In the flesh, but don't mind me, my nigga. Go ahead and finish telling Trappa what you had to say." I leaned back on the couch and looked up at him expectantly.

Trappa sighed and motioned for Uno to continue with the breaking news. "You heard the man. Spill the beans."

"Geno and a few of his Mobsters got caught up on the road riding dirty. On top of that, Venom just got caught slipping in traffic. Niggas sprayed his car up. Now he laid up in the hospital in critical condition."

"Damn bruh! I told Geno to stop moving recklessly. The police have been hot on our ass! And who the fuck caught my boy slippin'?" asked an angry Trappa.

Uno shrugged his shoulders. "Don't nobody know yet, bruh. Dizzy and the rest of the Mobsters in his camp trying to find out right now. Probably one of his out-of-town victims or some shit."

"Aight. Y'all niggas just be on high alert and move smart because we sitting on too much product to put a hold on business right now," Trappa expressed before picking his puppy back up.

Uno nodded his head in understanding before letting himself out.

"Damn shawty. I wasn't expecting him to say all that," I admitted sadly. This was the wrong time for that kind of heat.

Trappa took me by surprise when he let out a slight chuckle with a bright smile on his face.

"What's so funny?" I asked curiously. I could tell he wasn't smiling to hide the pain, he really found something funny. "This ain't the time to be laughing, bro."

"You got a lot to learn about this city... Just go home my nigga, we'll catch up. I got a business to manage in the meantime."

I didn't even argue because I knew how much Trappa had on his plate and I needed time to get my mind straight anyway, so I got up and left out of his spot.

It was dark, and cold, outside. The weather matched the energy of the city that night. It felt disturbing to my soul. All the passion and hope that I had for my mission in Fayetteville was dulled by uncertainty and uneasiness.

My car was parked right in front of Trappa's driveway. I showed up late, and it was even later now, but it seemed to be more people outside now. I knew everybody wasn't selling drugs, so the fact that all these people were outside at 1:30 in the morning, on a cold night, was weird to me.

I hopped in my car and proceeded up the hill towards the entrance of the community. I was vibing to my music and talking to Malika on the phone when I heard a strange noise.

Boc! Boc! Boc! Boc!

It wasn't until the third bullet was fired, which shattered my back window, that it actually hit me I was being shot at. I knew what a gunshot sounded like and I'd been shot at before, but I just couldn't believe that it was happening here and now.

Although I was caught by surprise, I recovered quickly. I don't even know what got into me, but I was a long way from the old me who was up under gunfire five years ago. Last time I hauled ass with my heart beating out of my chest. This time I parked my car, grabbed by Glock and popped out of the car shooting in the direction of the oncoming assault.

All I could hear was my mother's frail voice in my head. *"And you better not let them muthafuckas kill you out there in them streets."* I kept hearing her bark the same sentence over and over. Every time she repeated it, it seemed more intense and boosted me up even more. I had tunnel vision. At this point, I wasn't even scared. I was just determined to eliminate any threat to my life.

There were only two gunmen in my sights. I stood there like B-Rad from the movie *Malibu's most wanted* letting off shots at my opponents. One of them dodged my bullets by jumping behind a van, but the other stood toe to toe with me in a Mexican standoff.

"Aghhhh fuckkkk!" I spat as I stumbled back towards my car.

I felt a burning sensation on my side right below my rib cage and naturally pressed my free hand against the wound. I'd been shot and, all of a sudden, I was scared again. Luckily, my fear didn't hinder my trigger finger.

God had to be with me because I landed the last two bullets in my magazine into the gunman's torso before hopping back into the driver's seat of my car and speeding out of harm's way.

I escaped to the back streets and made it to Shaw Road safely on my way to Bragg Boulevard. I reached down on the floor to grab my phone to call Jay, but Malika was still on the phone. I had forgotten all about her.

"Hello! Rondo! Is that you?" She sounded worried and frantic.

"Yeah, it's me. I just got shot. Meet me at my spot," I informed before giving Jay a call, so he'd know what to be expecting by the time I got there.

Jay was in the driveway waiting on me to show up. I skid to a stop in my driveway a few feet away from him, put the car in park, and attempted to get out on my own, but Jay was right there by my side like always.

"What the fuck happened, nigga?" Jay asked after wrapping one of my arms around his neck and helping me out of the car.

"Niggas tried to whack me, nigga! What else?" I spat back, not really in the mood to talk. My side was hurting, and I was still in shock from the whole ordeal.

Once inside, I took all my clothes off from the waist up. Jay tried his best to clean the wound, but he was better at creating wounds than he was at cleaning them. He was far from knowing what he was doing, but Malika wasn't. Her mother was a doctor and had taught her various first aid techniques throughout her lifetime.

She showed up fifteen minutes after me. By that time my adrenaline went down and my bleeding did the same. She called a few minutes after I got inside and instructed Jay to pour alcohol on the wound and press a towel against it until she showed up.

The door wasn't locked, so she walked right in on us. I laid on the kitchen floor, in a small puddle of my blood, pressing the towel against the wound. I was looking at, Jay, who was sharing a very intense war story from when he was still living in Memphis before he went on the run.

"I don't mean to interrupt you guys' storytime, but this man needs medical attention," said Malika while setting up the medical supplies from inside of the bag she brought with her.

It turned out that I didn't even have a bullet inside of me. The bullet that struck me on the side took a big chunk of my flesh with it, leaving a nasty flesh wound which explained all the blood loss.

Malika got me all cleaned up, stitched up, and patched up within thirty minutes. She definitely knew what she was doing. "You know you could've just gone to the hospital. Getting shot isn't a crime in Fayetteville," she informed matter-a-factly while cleaning up the mess in the kitchen.

I struggled to my feet. I was blessed to have left the assassination attempt with just a flesh wound, but that didn't stop the fact that it still hurt like hell. "Nah, I don't need that type of attention on me right now."

"I guess... What now?" she asked while gazing at me with eyes full of concern and worry.

"Now, you go back home and wait for me to call you," I answered firmly. It bothered me to be pushing her away, but deep down, I knew it was the wise thing to do.

If she felt some type of way, she hid it very well. She finished cleaning up the mess in the kitchen, kissed me on my lips, and left the house without another word.

"You think she built for this shit?" Jay asked once she was gone.

I placed the carton of orange juice that I'd been drinking out of back on the counter. "If she's not, she will be when I get done with her," I vowed.

Chapter 15

The next morning, I laid in my big comfortable bed gathering my wild thoughts and emotions. I never knew why people laid on their backs looking up at the ceiling when they were in a dilemma, but I fell right in the same category. I stared at that ceiling as if the answer to all of my problems were about to appear on the wall in writing.

After I told Jay what happened to me, his first thought was to ride back into Ridge Park with guns blazing, but I reminded him that we didn't know who attempted to take my life. He then channeled his anger towards Trappa since he thought he had something to do with it, but I reminded him that we didn't have any evidence to support the accusation and I needed Trappa at the moment. I was at a big disadvantage.

Just like my mother's words sounded off in my head during the shootout, Trappa's words were now dangling in my mind. *"You got a lot to learn about this city."*

It wasn't just his words; it was the laugh that came before the sentence that didn't sit well with me either. There was something deeper in the works, but I couldn't see it because I wasn't in the loop. I was missing something. I had to talk to Venom. He was the only person outside of Jay that I trusted at this point. Everybody else was flaky.

The pain was there whenever I moved, but it wasn't unbearable. Malika patched me up something nice.

After deciding that it was urgent for me to talk to Venom as soon as possible, I got up and tried to make it happen.

"I'm not gon' lie, bro. You definitely surprised the hell out of me. I thought you was gon' be laid up like a lil' bitch for the next couple of days, but I see I was wrong," Jay cracked as I walked into the living room where he sat playing video games. "Where we going?"

I stuck a middle finger up at him. "We're going to the hospital to see Venom, so get ready."

***

I didn't even have to call anyone to find out where Venom was. The news reporter that covered the story on Venom's incident used Venom's real name in his report, so all I had to do was call around to locate him.

There were only three hospitals in the city and Venom was admitted into Cape Fear Valley Medical Center on Owen Drive. It was only a ten-minute drive away from my house, so it didn't take any time for us to pull up.

Jay didn't do hospitals and strongly refused to come in with me, so I slowly strolled inside solo. I had Jay help me wrap an ace bandage around my midsection before we left the house so I could maneuver a little painlessly.

The place was packed, and I must've been overdressed because I was attracting a generous amount of attention. When I was younger, I heard an OG once say that you'll always be able to tell when a rich nigga walked into a room because power would vibrate off of him. I couldn't help but wonder if those people felt power radiating off of me.

The receptionist at the front desk was a heavyset middle-aged black lady. She stared at me curiously as I approached the desk. "How are you doing ma'am? I'm here to visit one of the patients here."

I gave her Venom's government name and she sent me to room 316 where Venom was being held. She also informed me that he had just got out of surgery not too long ago, so the doctors probably wouldn't let me see him. I hopped on the elevator anyway. I had to try.

When I got off the elevator, I saw a group of people who had to be some type of family to Venom. I'd been introduced to his baby mother, Prima, so I knew who she was. She sat down with her head resting on some old lady with her leg shaking frantically when she looked up and seen me approaching. She stood up and took steps towards me.

"I'm sorry for all the trouble," I offered before giving her a quick hug.

She waved me off dismissively. "I've been going through this same shit forever. I should be saying the same to you. I heard niggas tried to take your head off last night, but you handled that shit accordingly."

She took me by surprise with her response. I didn't see that coming. "Yeah, that's why I need to talk to Venom like right now. I know he just got out of surgery and all, but you think he can talk?"

"He only took two in the leg, one in the arm, and one in the chest. If it wasn't for the chest shot, we wouldn't even be in here. He be in here so much; all the doctors know his name. He sleeping. That's the only reason why I'm not in there right now, but I know he'll want to hear from you," she informed giving me her blessing to go to his room.

Venom must've felt just as paranoid as I did because he had two real professional security guards standing guard at his door, and they looked like they meant business. If he felt that he needed security, I knew for a fact that I did. That was the first thing on my list once I left the hospital.

The guards frisked me before allowing me entrance into the room. Venom laid on his back with the bed propping him up. The

TV was on, but it was on mute. It was very quiet in the room, so I could see how he heard me come in.

"I told y'all to let me sleep, man," he spat in a low voice with his eyes still closed.

I took two steps closer to the bed. "This Rondo, big bro. Prima told me you was sleep, but I need to chop it up with you real quick. It's urgent."

His eyes popped open, and he looked up at me with a slow smile. "If it ain't John Wick Jr.!"

He seemed excited to see me, and I didn't ignore the fact that he named me after the assassin from the famous movie. I've seen it in his eyes. He looked at me like a proud mentor.

"I see you got jokes, and I also see news travel fast around this muthafucka," I retorted with a straight face.

"Lighten up my nigga. You just beat the odds, once again," he advised, ironically.

My face instantly crumbled up into a mug. "I'm not you, Venom. I'm not used to niggas gunning at me. I don't take shit like that lightly. Something got to give, and that's on the 4's. I'm not gon' let that shit slide."

"My situation was an assassination attempt, hands down, but yours was more like a test," he hypothesized.

His face was now just as serious as mines, so he had to believe what he was saying. "A test! What the fuck? Please don't tell me you was in on that shit, bro." I really wanted him to deny the accusation. I *needed* him to.

To my relief, he shook his head no. "Hell no... This shit bigger than you and me. I told you this city was fucked up. Just give me a lil' time to connect some dots and I'll let you know something."

"So, what I'm supposed to do in the meantime? Because I don't trust anybody right now. How the hell I'm supposed to help a camp full of niggas that I don't trust?" I asked seriously.

It took him a few moments to answer. "Just look at the bright side, you passed the test. Niggas gon' respect you now that they know you're not a bitch. You know what you signed up for, and you still got a job to do out here, so suck that shit up, put yo' emotions in check, and act like that shit didn't even phase you. That's how you throw them off. That's how you last."

"What about you?" I asked curiously. "Who the hell tried to kill you?"

"The rumor going around is that it was one of my enemies from out of town, but I think it was one of my own... Keep that lil' piece of information to yourself though. Just keep doing you," he insisted.

I promised to stay in touch before leaving him to get his rest. I felt more at ease after my visit with him. I had to keep my game face on and continue handling business.

Chapter 16

"Man, I'm trying to tell you, that's a sucka ass move right there. Who you think you is nigga? El Chapo? You don't need no damn professional security. The only reason Venom hired them guards is because he don't trust his own niggas and he's not able to protect himself right now," Jay informed heatedly.

When I got back in the car with him, I ran down all the new information I got from Venom and shared my thoughts on bringing in hired security. Like always, he gave me his honest feedback.

"I hear what you saying, Jay. Despite what you or anybody else think, I cherish my life. I got a lot of shit I want to do before I'm laying up under that dirt, my nigga. Can't let these miserable ass niggas kill me," I countered matter-a-factly.

I looked over at, Jay, who was shaking his head in disagreement with clenched teeth. "I'm not gon' let these niggas kill you, nigga! You really insulting me right now, Rondo. The only reason you got shot is because yo' dumb ass decided to leave the house without me. You know how I give it up!"

I now had my eyes on traffic, but I was zoned out. Completely lost in my thoughts and taking Jay's words into consideration.

"Listen, I understand yo' reason for wanting to hire some security, but if you ain't never listened to me, you need to do it now bro. That same respect you just gained last night gon' go right out the window when these folks see you walking around everywhere with some ex-military-ass nigga. If you feel like you gon' need reinforcements, then you need to go grab a shooter from East Atlanta."

I looked back over at him knowingly. "You know damn well I don't trust them niggas neither."

"It's different now, bro. You not trusting them while we in ATL is understandable, but if you bring one of them all the way out here, they gon' be on an island just like us. We gon' be the closest thing to home, and they gon' stick close. I'm telling you," he assured.

"I see you got it all figured out, huh?"

"I'll let you have that hustling shit, but when it comes to this warfare, you know I'm an expert, dawg," Jay informed proudly.

I nodded my head in understanding. This was his field, and he was making sense, so I took his advice into consideration.

About fifteen minutes later, we were pulling up into Ridge Park. I had the element of surprise because I was driving the Escalade that came with the house in the garage. There was some serious work to be done on my car and I was definitely upset about that, but I couldn't complain too much because the holes in the car could've been inside of me.

The hood was alive as usual, and that's just the way I was hoping it would be. I wanted everybody to see me stand tall in the same spot a nigga tried to drop me just the night before.

I pulled up in front of Trappa's trailer, and it was just my luck that he was outside amongst a group of Mobsters. They all stopped what they were doing to watch the truck that had pulled up.

Jay hopped out first with his Mac11 in hand, and just stood there as I took my time climbing out of the driver's seat with my Glock in hand. The pain in my midsection would take a little getting used to, but I could deal until the wound healed. I wasn't going to let it stop anything. Business must go on. I had my game face on as I walked up to Trappa, who looked like me like he was seeing a ghost.

"What's poppin' y'all? What it's looking like today? Surprised the police ain't riding around this bitch all deep and shit," I said as I walked up to them with Jay right by my side.

Trappa stood on the wooden porch that was attached to his trailer staring at me openmouthed, but he recovered quickly before jogging down the stairs towards me. "They was out here last night, but you know how this shit goes. They pulled up and pulled off. They don't give a fuck about us out here, but fuck all that. You good? I got news of what happened when you left. I was calling yo' phone, but you never answered."

"Don't I look good, nigga? I'm just wondering who the fuck was stupid enough to try some shit like that." I scanned the small crowd of Mobsters grimly as I said that, and I saw something that I didn't see before. It was fear. Venom was right.

Trappa shrugged his shoulders. "It had to be some other niggas because you know ours definitely wouldn't do no shit like that."

"Other niggas in one of *our* hoods? I don't understand that," I said through squinted eyes, not even trying to hide the suspicion in my voice.

"I mean, it's a big hood and it was dark bruh. It really could've been anybody, but I'm on top of it. We definitely gon' find them pussy niggas."

I nodded my head slowly. "I'll take that for now, but anyway. I had told Rod to meet me out here for a sit down earlier, but I got last-minute plans, so let him know we gon' have to reschedule. I'll holla at you. Keep this shit in line out here in the meantime since you got *other niggas* running around here with death wishes and shit," I said before walking off.

I was driving out of the neighborhood when I looked over at Jay and saw him smiling at me devilishly. "What nigga?" I asked with a weird expression etched on my face.

"You handled that muthafuckin' business like a gangsta, nigga, that's what! I'm proud of you, shawty," he informed happily.

I couldn't suppress my smile if I wanted to. It was rare that I saw Jay that excited and full of life, so I had to enjoy the moment. "That shit was gangsta, wasn't it?" I asked jokingly.

It was times like this that I wish Jay wasn't on the run. Not only was he my protector, but basically he was also my best friend these days, and I didn't even want to imagine how shit would be without him.

Chapter 17

I walked into the Footlocker inside the mall and instantly spotted Malika assisting a man with his shopping. I just stood there in the middle of the store openly staring at her until she eventually looked up and noticed me.

She did a double take when she recognized me and kindly excused herself from the customer before walking towards me and Jay. "Why aren't you getting rest? I know you only had a flesh wound, but I know it's still causing you pain. It hasn't even been a full twenty-four hours." Her concern for me was genuine, I could tell that much.

I waved her off though. "I'll be fine, baby girl. Don't worry about that. I really just wanted to see your face before I left."

"Awwwwww! You're too sweet, but where are you going? You not moving back to Atlanta, are you?" she asked sadly with pouty eyes.

"Nah, but I am visiting for a few days." I pulled her in for a hug and gave her a quick peck on the lips, careful not to put to do too much in her workplace. "And I need to talk to you when I get back."

"You can hang around about thirty minutes until my break if it's important," she informed.

"It is important, but it can wait until I get back."

She gave me a brief lecture about staying safe, and I left out of the store. She meant something to me as well, and I was afraid to gain the type of feelings for her where I would be scared to lose her.

Before we hopped on the road, I had to stop at the house so Jay could help me clean my wound and change my bandage. Malika warned me to keep it clean and to take good care of it because deep wounds were always a high risk for infection.

As I stood there while Jay wrapped the ace bandage around my waist, I thought about how much effort it took me to operate the truck throughout Fayetteville, then thought about me trying to make it all the way to Atlanta. I immediately cringed at the thought and made a sudden change of plans.

***

Twelve hours later, we exited the train at an Amtrak train station on Peachtree Road. I stopped to perform a painful stretch while releasing a yawn that turnt into a growl due to the pain.

Despite my pain, I felt a little better that I got some sleep during the ride. I needed that idle time to formulate a few survival and financial strategies. That attempt on my life changed the game for me and made things way more complicated, but I was still here breathing for a reason, so I kept my eyes on the bright side and kept pushing.

"There that nigga go right there," Jay informed looking over in Stevo's direction.

Stevo stood in the middle of the platform, accompanied by two firm looking Mobsters, glued to his phone.

We walked over towards him and met up with him. I had to check in with Allo before visiting ATL since I was now officially an outsider, and he sent Stevo to meet me personally.

"4's up," Stevo and I greeted in unison as we embraced each other.

"What brings you back so fast?" he asked as we walked towards the exit.

I glanced over at him. "Is that question coming from you or Allo?

He laughed at the question. "You're not a threat to Allo no more, he don't care about you no more. Me, on the other hand, I'm curious."

"Just a lil' homesick. Gone do a lil' shopping, hit the strip club, and kick it for a few days before going back to my post," I lied for a reason.

There was no need for me to reveal anything to Stevo. I fucked with him and considered him as an ally, but I still had to play my cards close. Just felt like the smartest thing to do at the moment.

When we made it outside to the parking lot, the Mobsters hopped into the Escalade beside Stevo's BMW, and we hopped in the car with Stevo. He tried to kick it, but I was forced to turn him down.

I made him drop us off at a car rental place nearby, where I rented a white Range Rover. Shortly after, I checked us into The Westin Peachtree Plaza on Peachtree Street, but we didn't stay long because we hit the road as soon as the room was bought. No need in checking it out, we both knew exactly what the room looked like.

I set up three very important meetings within a twenty-four-hour time span. I wanted to square away business as quickly as possible, so I could wind down and relax for the remaining days of the mini vacation.

First in line was the rich white boy, Cliff. He stood in a silk gold Versace robe watching me through wide eyes as I struggled to climb onto the barstool in his massive kitchen. "Aghhhh! What's good my boy?"

"I should be asking you the same, bro'. You alright over there?" he asked in concern. "Pulled a muscle in your back or something?"

I shook my head with a grimace. "I wish, nigga. Niggas tried to bust my head last night and I ended up getting shot man. Hurt like hell."

"Nooooooo!" I had his full attention now. "You alright?"

I looked at him blankly. "Nigga, do it look like I'm alright? I just got shot and my girl had to get the bullet out then patch me up. My own Mobsters trying to kill me out of jealousy, and the FEDs are hot on my ass, shawty. Shit ugly."

"Damnnnn man! That's rough right there."

"That's how shit gets when you get in the game. This the part the rappers be leaving out... What the hell you been on since I've been gone?"

He shrugged his shoulders. "Just basically partying and riding my dirt bikes. I told you I was going to leave the game alone when you left, bro'. I never tried to cop from anyone else."

"What else you tell me before I left, Cliff?" I asked with a raised eyebrow.

"That my loyalty would always be yours, and if you ever needed anything to let me know," he answered without hesitation.

"Exactly... You swore your loyalty and presented a door for me to open," I retorted matter-a-factly. "You know I don't take shit like that lightly right?"

He nodded his head understandingly.

"Alright. With that being said, right now I'm testing your loyalty and I'm attempting to open that door."

Cliff looked a little confused but interested. "Like in what way? What do I have to do? Talk to me, brodie. You know I trust you completely."

I purposely made a dramatic pause to build suspense, and I knew it was working. "I'm gon' give you what you want. I'm gon' stamp you Dilluminati directly up under me, but it's shit that comes with that."

I've seen, and felt, the excitement shoot off of him. "Bro! You know that's all I ever want to do is become DG official."

"First off, you gon' have to pay your dues of $400,000, but not cash or nothing. I'm gon' need it transferred into my personal bank account within four days. Then you're gonna have to get up off yo' ass and do something productive with yourself. You'll be an asset to my camp, so no more illegal activities for you. You're out. Since you like promoting and partying so much, you need to buy a rave club and turn it up or something. I don't care, as long as it's legit and profitable," I informed while looking him straight in his ocean blue eyes.

He closed the distance between us and sat in the chair next to mines. "Seriously bro'? That's it? I do that and I'll be able to go get my tattoo?" he asked, sounding years younger.

I shook his head with a chuckle. "Yeah, man. You'll be stamped."

"I can get you the money in four hours, bro. I'm down!" He was officially a part of something he felt was bigger than life, and I could tell it filled him with joy. He was smiling from ear-to-ear.

I wrapped the meeting up after giving Cliff my bank info' and applying a few more stipulations and ground rules to our arrangement.

"Why you lie to him in there about what happened to you? Wasn't no bullet in you, and the FEDs probably don't even know yo' name yet. You was trying to scare him, huh?" Jay stated, then asked curiously.

I shook my head in disagreement. "Hell nah, I don't try to scare niggas, that's your swag. I'm a finesser, bro. I was trying to impress him, and as you can see, the shit worked."

He leaned back in the passenger's seat and nodded his head while looking out the window. The fact that he had nothing to say showed that I was right. I had the juice.

Next, was the world-famous superstar, Ronte, in the flesh.

By the time we pulled up to the Def Jam studio in Atlantic Station, I was dazed, thinking about the movie my life had turned out to be. For some reason, my success never really hit me until now. That meeting with Cliff was a major turning point in my life. I had leveled up like *Super Mario*.

We sat in the studio's parking lot smoking on some Kush Stevo dropped on me before we departed.

"This nigga got us fucked up, shawty! We've been waiting on him for a whole thirty minutes. I don't care nothing about that Hollywood shit, I'll tell Ronte about himself," Jay barked grimly.

I laughed as I put the joint out in the door's ashtray. "Nah shawty, just chill! We ain't waiting on him, he waiting on us lil' nigga," I informed confidently before opening the door releasing a humongous thick cloud of weed smoke out of the Range Rover.

The two professionally dressed security guards openly eyed us as we approached the entrance.

"Name?" The bigger Caucasian guard asked while looking down at the guest list on his iPad.

"DG Rondo," I answered.

He tapped the pad while nodding his head up-and-down. "Okay, you're good."

"You a new artist, or something?" The younger African American guard asked me, a little friendlier than his coworker.

I shook my head slowly. "Nah, big dawg. I'm the nigga they be rapping about," I informed matter-a-factly before entering the building.

They had a beautiful lobby and an all-female staff that was even more beautiful. This was a real industry studio. Only A and B-list celebrities recorded in studios like this.

A well-built assistant escorted us to our destination on the second floor. I expected to walk into a full studio with weed smoking and bottle popping, but I wasn't expecting to see Ronte in the studio solo playing with his kid daughter. He wasn't even all dressed up, or nothing. He had on designer jeans and a Ralph Lauren white tee. He didn't even wear any jewelry. He was chilling for real.

"Fours up, twin! I see you in here vibing with the offspring. I respect that." I saluted upon walking into the room.

Jay and I dapped him up before taking a seat on the other end of the wraparound leather sofa.

"Yeah shawty. I can't do that Rockstar shit every day. Got to slow shit down sometimes and maintain balance," He responded wisely.

I nodded my head in agreement with a smirk on my face. That's why I fucked with the nigga. Not because he was rich, I was rich. Not because he was famous, I could buy fame if I wanted it. I fucked with the nigga because he actually made sense when he opened his mouth. He motivated everyone around him along with his millions of fans. He wasn't considered a rapper; he was more of a preacher. I was in a personal meeting with one of the most important men in Dilluminati.

"I feel that. Just keep up the good work. You making a real difference out here, to be honest," I encouraged sincerely. I looked up to the young nigga. He was definitely far beyond his years.

"I appreciate that, but you a real motivation. You out here running laps around vets that have been doing this shit for decades and breaking records. That's why I started fucking with you. You doing the same thing I'm doing in the rap game, but the only difference is you're in a different game. Either way, you remind me of myself," he assured while playing tug-of-war with his daughter and her doll.

I smiled involuntarily at the praise. "Don't gas me up, shawty, and speaking of gassing niggas up. I really called this sit down because I wanted to chop it up with you personally about that young nigga, Manny. You think he really that good how you say?"

He nodded in head quickly. "Hell, fuck yeah! That lil' nigga got what it takes. I know a star when I see one. I was just listening to his shit in the truck on my way over here, on the 4's."

"You know I'm a made-man now, so I'm really responsible for everybody in my camp. if I'm gon' let him rap, you got to bring him out personally. I don't want him to get signed yet because I want him to work for this shit. It's already too easy for the nigga, so you got to feed him the game slowly."

"I know exactly what you mean, and I agree with you. I got this. I know exactly what to do," said Ronte, excitedly.

I took a deep breath. This was another power move for me because I was about to transform Manny into a neighborhood hero. I was his hero, so that would automatically make me their hero as well. Manny didn't even know he was about to help me accomplish my mission that much faster. He was now officially the Chosen One.

***

Last, but definitely not least, I was set to meet with one of the most ruthless men in the city. His name was DG Mazi, and his name was ringing bells in the streets.

He was the man I chose to come to for security. He ran a camp full of the most reckless Mobsters in all of Dilluminatit. They were notorious for their ruthlessness. Mazi was a very busy man, but I was now considered royalty, so he made time for me.

He was one of those types who had never left the hood, and never would, so of course, we were meeting in Sun Valley Apartments on Bouldercrest Avenue in East Atlanta.

A group of Baby Mobsters played a game of concrete football in the middle of the parking lot while Mazi and a few Mafiosos lounged around a parked Escalade watching them.

I found a parking spot and got out since Mazi wasn't showing any indication that he was about to walk to my truck. Jay and I walked across the parking lot towards them.

"Fours up," I greeted as I dapped Mazi up.

He was a little taller than me, but he was way bigger, like he could've been a personal trainer if he chose. "All the time... What can I help you with dawg? Who you need whacked?" he asked casually like it was a regular question.

The Mafiosos that were keeping him company suddenly fell back onto the sidewalk out of earshot, so Mazi and I could talk business in private.

"It's not nothing like that big dawg. I need you for something else. I just got transferred to a North Carolina camp, but I don't trust them niggas, so I'm here to see if you'll lend me at least two of your shooters," I informed.

Mazi laughed in my face as if I was a joke, and I didn't like that shit. At the same time, I was prepared for him to react that way. I motioned for Jay to pass me the Nike book bag off of his back. I grabbed the bag and offered it to Mazi.

Mazi accepted the bag, zipped it open, and took a peek inside. "Damn! I see you ain't come to play, huh?" he asked with wide eyes after releasing a low whistle.

"Nah, I'm not into games, big bro. I'm strictly about my business and I'm also strict on safety which is why I'm standing in front of you now."

He pursed his lips together and took a deep breath through his nose. "You said you was trying to borrow two of my Mobsters, but judging by all this money in the bag, it looks like you trying to buy them."

Due to the fact that I was just another street nigga less than six months ago, and still adapting to my newfound prestige in the world, it was easy for me to forget who I was. I was on the same level as Mazi, so I had to act like it. "Look. This lame ass nigga, Allo, done sent me out there with all them country ass niggas. Niggas just tried to whack me on the road solo, but fortunately, I handled my business accordingly. I'm here right now, but the same bullet that grazed me on the side could've hit me in the heart." I slapped the left side of my chest for emphasis. "All I got is my shooter Jay right here. That's $100,000 in that bag. I need two thoroughbreds on my team. Plain and simple."

He peered into my soul for an uncomfortable amount of time before speaking. "Say no more. I got two OG's for you too... They'll look at it as a promotion too, so you need to take good care of their pockets and they'll forever take good care of you."

I waved him off nonchalantly. "Nah, I can't do that because their money ain't gon' be able to fit in their pockets. Everybody around me making bag money, my nigga."

"Got to respect it when a nigga poppin' cash talk," said Mazi before reaching out for a handshake to seal the deal.

Chapter 18

"I mean, I don't get no bad vibe from them or nothing. I know they official because they were in Mazi's camp, so I feel like you did the right thing. We just got to get to know 'em so we can gain trust for 'em." Jay said while sitting at the dining table next to me.

We were in South DeKalb Mall's food court watching the pair of mobsters Mazi gave me.

They were actually a married couple. They were both dark-skinned, but that was their only physical resemblance. Drama was a tall chubby dude with a curly tempted fro' like mines, but a little lower. Unity was very short and skinny. From my knowledge, they were both in their mid-thirties and basically inseparable.

Mazi informed me that Drama put in some very important work for him and that he owed Drama a big favor. Rolling with me, compared to the dysfunctional family they came from, was like a blessing in comparison so I can see why Mazi handed them over. He assured me that they both were more than capable of keeping me safe out in Fayetteville, and of course, I took his word for it.

They made their way back over to the table with their food. "We ain't got no choice but to trust them. They're family now," I responded truthfully.

***

Two days later, I returned back to my post in Fayetteville feeling a little better about my situation. I went to Atlanta and moved some important pieces on the chessboard.

When we got to the house, I smiled brightly when I saw Malika's purple Jaguar in my driveway. I see she wasn't bullshitting when she said she was waiting for me to come back.

Once in the house, I told Jay to go ahead and show Drama and Unity their room while I caught up with Malika in my room.

After removing her own coat, she helped me take off mines so I wouldn't have to struggle. "What's that in your face?" she asked while squinting at the new dermal piercing in my face an inch away from my right eyeball.

I removed my hood from over my head. "That's a $5,000 diamond in my face, that's what it is. Like it?" I asked and leaning down so she could see it more clearly.

"Yeah. It's different and actually cute on you," she admitted before closing the distance between us and placing her big glossed lips onto mines softly.

I was starting to feel something other than the pain on my side rising. It was something about this girl here that made me want to protect her from the world. She wasn't average and I felt like she really reached the requirements of being with a nigga of my caliber.

I pulled her closer as we continued to kiss passionately. My hands ended up on her lower back and I started shifting her over to the bed. If I wasn't in pain, I probably would've carried her.

I sat down on the bed and she climbed on top of me. "You trying to seduce me, mister?" she whispered sweetly into my ear sending a small surge of vibrations to my, already erect, penis.

"Shitttt, you the one that kissed me first. I'm just going with the flow," I retorted smoothly.

She pulled herself back, so she could sit up and look at me. "You know why I'm here right now."

"Because you missed me, I hope?" I asked while raising a curious brow.

She slapped me playfully on my shoulder. "That goes without asking. You know the effect you have on my life, but that's not the only reason I'm here. You said you needed to talk to me when you got back, so here I am."

"Damn, girl. You be on it. I definitely did say I needed to talk to you, and I do. It's just an understanding that I'm looking for," I ensured.

"Talk to me, Rondo. Tell me exactly what it is you feel like you need to say," she requested pleadingly.

She'd been waiting all these days to see what I had to say, and I could tell she was getting impatient. The fact that my words, and thoughts, were so important to her held weight with me.

"Alright, look. I know you want to wait before sex and take shit slow. I respect that to the fullest, but I'm trying to see if you'll respect my choice behind that."

She cocked her head to the side slightly. "And what's your choice behind that?"

"You know I don't have no family, and I already shared how bad I want one. That incident a few days ago made me realize that I don't have all the time in the world, so I'm trying to get started right away," I delivered the blow as soft as I could.

She stared down at me looking like she was in deep thought. When the silence began to get weird, I was about to say something else, but she cut me off. "So, let me get this right. You're trying to have kids, like right now?"

I nodded my head. "Exactly... I plan on finding a fit mother for my child that reaches my personal list of requirements and paying her to have my baby for me."

"Wow! So, you want to pay a random woman to have your baby? That's very unusual," she asked and stated matter-a-factly with a look of disapproval.

"No, I don't want to, it feels more like a need to me."

She got up off of me and stood up before pacing the floor with both hands on her hips. It looked like she was making the most important decision in her life. I didn't disturb her, just sat up on the bed watching her go through the motions in silence.

"Can't you just wait a little while longer?" She stopped in her tracked and faced me. "You're so obsessed with the number forty-four, right? Give me that many days and I'll have an answer by then. This is a lot for me. I'm not used to your world, and I'm not used to you, so just bear with me. You see I'm trying to keep up with you as best I can."

I nodded my head up-and-down approvingly. She was trying to keep up with me, and I adored that. I adored her for showing that she didn't want to lose me, and for making sacrifices for me.

I reached out to pull her back down on top of me. "It's a bet. I'm not gon' let you down. Just follow my lead. I got us!"

Chapter 19

I woke up the next day from a deep sleep feeling discombobulated. It was taking me longer than usual to come to my senses. It was my body telling me I needed more sleep, but my mind told me to open my eyes, so that's what I did.

I've been waking up to mild depression ever since I was a teenager, it was always hard to fight, but now that I had a real purpose in life, it wasn't so hard. I actually had something to live for. Like *really* live for.

I used to dream, and wake up to a hard reality, but now I couldn't tell the dream from real life. It was definitely a remarkable experience.

I looked down at Malika, who laid in my arms comfortably. She was the newest addition to my dream, and I was grateful. She snored lightly with her head on my chest and her arms wrapped around my body. I moved her arm slowly so I wouldn't wake her and got out of the bed and head to the shower.

"Where are you going?" she asked in a groggy tone while wiping the cold from her eyes.

"I've got business to handle," I answered while looking down at her.

"I thought we were going to spend the day together," she stated disappointedly.

"We are," I informed before continuing to my walk to the bathroom.

There was a popular skating rink called *Blast Off* on Bragg Boulevard, but it also turned into a nightclub after hours. I heard a few locals mention the place, so I asked Venom about the spot and he told me it was just one of the places to be in the city.

It was around 11:30 pm when I walked through the front doors with my small entourage. I was dressed flashy in a sparkling silver

101

Givenchy varsity jacket and high-top Alexander McQueen shoes to match, so I expected the attention I was now receiving.

My name was already trending in the area since I first touched down in the city, but now my face was starting to get recognized as well. I caught a few open stares and charged it as part of the game. I would have to deal with the local fame just how I dealt with the money, carefully. Both could be used to my advantage, so it was to be appreciated and embraced.

I walked through the place like I was part owner. I was vibing hard to the music, feeling myself, and I was righteous for doing so. I was doing what my mother wanted. I was enjoying life.

"Look, babe! They're about to start the money machine up," Malika informed while tugging on my arm pulling me towards it.

A small woman got inside of the box-shaped machine with a huge smile on her face. A large group of spectators gathered around as she stood there waiting for the wind in the machine to be cut on so she could grab as many hundred-dollar bills as possible.

The machine was brought to life, the crowd cheered the lady on as she reached and grabbed at all the hundred-dollar bills flying in the machine.

I bent down and spoke into Malika's ear, "You want to go next?"

"I can't. They only do one person per night," she informed without taking her eyes off the action.

After that, we headed over to the food section. It was literally its own section too. There was a long counter with four open registers serving four lines of people.

My side was starting to throb irritatingly, and I knew I wasn't going to be able to stand in the line for that long, so we gave Drama and Unity our orders before grabbing a seat at one of the dining tables.

The food section was more lit than the main floor, so I could see people staring at me more clearly. I stared a few people back in the eye, but I brushed it off for the most part.

When I saw Manny walk into the food section with two females on his hips, I smiled inwardly. The key to all my problems had just arrived. I told him to meet me here. I figured it would be a perfect place, and time, for me to chop it up with the youngin.

"Wassup, lil' nigga? Who you got with you?" I asked curiously while openly scanning the two young women with him.

He looked at the pecan thick girl to his left. "This my baby mama right here." He looked at the elegant redbone to his right. "And this my big sister."

I nodded at both of them. They nodded back.

"Aight, that's wassup. I really ain't trying to hold you up, this ain't gon' take long." I reached my hand out towards, Malika, who dug in her Fendi purse and came out with a diamond-crusted DG chain. "I had a lil' talk with DG Ronte, and he decided to take you up under his wing. This chain came from him personally."

Manny was openmouthed, and it looked like he was in a state of shock, but that didn't stop him from reaching out and grabbing the chain as if I would change my mind. "He gon' get me signed?" he asked excitingly.

I nodded my head up-and-down. "Yeah, you'll get signed eventually, but not at this exact moment. You've got to get groomed first... I'm about to shout you out on my Instagram page, and by the time you get home, Ronte should have been shouted you out on his page. I don't know when, but he'll be in contact with you soon so y'all can do a song together, and the rest is basically history."

"Are you serious right now? *My* brother is about to be famous!" his uniquely attractive sister asked interestingly.

I nodded my head for an answer.

"Damnnnn! I thought he was just talking shit, but damnnnn!" she admitted.

Manny flashed a big crooked smile. "As you can see, big bro', ain't nobody believe the jet was gon' to take off until it got in the sky," he retorted before dodging a playful punch his sister sent his way.

I let him and his company join us for dinner. It was sort of a celebration, so I tried my best to enjoy it with him instead of talking business all night.

I couldn't do too much due to my wound, but that didn't stop me from having fun. I really enjoyed Malika's company. We were kicking it in our VIP section when I told her to get on the floor so she could skate. She didn't want to leave me out, but I assured her that I couldn't skate anyway and wouldn't be missing anything.

Manny was dancing in the section with his baby mother, Jay was dancing with Manny's sister, and Drama was on the floor skating with Unique and Malika, keeping a watchful eye on both of them.

I was sitting down on the circular couch vibing to one of Ronte's songs that were being played while texting Ronte about Manny when I felt my bladder all of a sudden. I'd been sipping on a large cup of Sprite for the past few hours and it had finally caught up with me.

Jay was in his zone having fun, and I didn't want to disturb him because I rarely saw him let loose, so I slipped out of the section on my way to the restroom. I was in a public place, so I wasn't really worried about anything happening to me.

The bathroom was big with a big man dressed in the Blast Off uniform sitting inside by the door to assist the attendants. I nodded at him for a greeting and proceeded to one of the urinals to relieve myself.

There was soft R&B music playing in the background, and it was soothing. I was relaxed until I finished pissing and turned around to wash my hands. The bathroom man wasn't sitting down anymore. He stood up in front of the bathroom door blocking my exit while glaring at me murderously.

He looked like a bald-headed version of Buster Rhymes. "Ain't nobody else in here. It's just me and you baby girl," he informed in a deep voice as I looked over at the line of open toilet stalls.

"Baby girl?" I asked in confusion. "What's going on right here, shawty?"

Bald head smiled widely. "Yeahhhh! Baby girl, nigga! If it was up to me, I would drag you in one of them toilet stalls and turn you into a lil' baby girl, but it's not up to me."

"Oh yeahhhh? Who is it up to then?" I asked matter-a-factly as I drew the pocketknife from my inside jacket pocket. Security wouldn't let us in with guns, but I managed to slip past with my knife, and I was grateful.

Bald head made a show of loudly cracking his thick neck and big knuckles before charging at me like an angry bull.

I braced myself for the impact, gripping my knife with a gorilla grip. I wasn't a fighter and I doubted if I had a chance with this nigga on a regular day, so the fact that I was already wounded put me at a major disadvantage. I was scared as fuck, but I couldn't let this big gay ass nigga kill me.

He came forward with a hard kick that I barely sidestepped. The pain in my side was definitely slowing me down. When he spun back around catching me with a backhanded blow, I knew it was only a matter of time before he got the best of me, so I had to think of something fast.

I took two big painful backward steps away from him to buy me a little time to recover from the blow, but he wasn't having it.

"Ughhhhhhh! He charged me again, but this time I couldn't sidestep shit because he had both arms extended to the fullest while charging. He was obviously trying to tackle me.

Within a millisecond before impact, I sucked up the pain, and dove to the ground up under his arms causing him to run into the hard granite wall. He recovered much quicker than me. I was still on the ground struggling the get up while he was on his feet slowly walking over to me, like Jason in a scary movie without the knife.

"Come on, shawty! Whatever they paying you I'll double!" I promised desperately. I was on my hands and knees attempting to get on my feet when he sent a crucial kick to my midsection sending me back to the ground in unimaginable pain. "Ahhhhhhhhhh! Please. I can't... go out like this." Tears were flowing down my eyes and it was hard for me to breathe. I never felt pain like this before in my young life. The stitches from my wound popped, and I started bleeding all over again.

He bent down and picked my knife up off the floor that I dropped upon the kick. "This ain't about the money, young buck. I would've done this job for free just because you an outsider."

As he got down on one knee preparing to cause me more damage, I closed my eyes and began to send a prayer up to God, but he must've read my mind because someone started banging on the door just in time. "Yooo, Rondo! You in there, shawty?"

I recognized that voice instantly. I've never been so happy to hear Jay's voice in my life. Bald Head turned around towards the door out of instinct. I took the opportunity to suck up all the pain and yell at the top of my lungs to make sure I was heard over the music. "Yoooooooo!"

"Time for me to finish..." Bald head began to say, but I surprised him with an attack of my own.

I don't know how I did it, but the adrenaline that I mustered up from the realization that I was about to lose my life gave me the strength to push myself up far enough to reach Bald Head's face. I could've done a number of things, but I just psyched-out and bit on his huge nose.

I knew I was biting him hard because I began to taste his salty blood in my mouth within a matter of seconds. I turned into a pit bull and started shaking while growling.

"Oooooooh! Oooooh! Ohhhhhh!" he shouted in a suddenly high-pitched voice. It wasn't until then that I noticed I had a handful of his nuts in a gorilla grip as well. Once again, I don't know what had gotten into me, but I'm glad it did because he definitely was going to kill me.

After seven hard kicks on the bathroom door, it flew open and Jay came rushing in with Manny right behind him.

They saw me on the floor with Bald Head and rushed over to assist me. Manny helped me up while Jay started pounding Bald Head's face in. He picked up the knife off the floor and attempted to use it, but I stopped him before he could strike. "Noo! We need that fuck nigga alive, bro."

Malik D. Rice

Chapter 20

My first thought was to shut the whole skating rink down, and Jay was with the bullshit like always, but luckily Manny still had his head-on. He suggested that we take Bald Head out of the side door, so we could handle him accordingly without drawing heat.

I appreciated his piece of mind, but I let him know there was no *we* because he didn't need to be mixed up in this shit. He needed to be in the studio, so I ordered him to take his folks and go his own way.

Later on that morning, I was laying on my couch as Malika stitched my side back up. I saw it in her face that she wanted to say something, but she must've seen it in my face that I wasn't in the mood for her two cents at the moment. Another attempt was made on my life, and I was pissed off in the worst way.

"All done. I'm about to go grab some supplies to clean it," she informed while standing to her feet.

I struggled to my feet after her. "Nah, I'll handle the rest. Thank you shawty, but I need you to go home. I'll hit you up soon."

She broke eye contact with me and shifted her eyes to the ground for a few seconds before making eye contact again. "Okay. Just don't push me away. I know these are difficult times for you, but I'm here for all of that. My concern for you is growing by the minute."

I kissed her with my swollen lip and sent her on her way after assuring her that I would be in touch. It wasn't that I didn't trust her because I actually did, I just felt that it would be safer for her to be away from me for the time being until I figured out who was trying to kill me and terminated them.

After Malika was gone, I walked into the kitchen where Bald Head was tied to a chair knocked out unconscious.

"Man, I walked in that muthafucka and Rondo had a mouth full of that niggas nose like Mike Tyson and a hand full of the nigga's balls like Katt Williams off of *Friday After Next!* My boy wasn't going out bad, shawty!" Jay told Drama and Unique, filling them in on the action they missed out on.

They all burst out into laughter, and it only pissed me off even more. "Oh, y'all think this shit a joke huh? Niggas out there trying to take my whole muthafuckin' head off, and y'all in here giggling and shit!" I barked despite the pain I received from doing so.

They all straightened up upon hearing my sharp voice and viewing my cold expression.

"Nah, I was just..."

I cut Jay off mid-sentence. "Fuck all that! Wake this bitch ass nigga up," I commanded sternly.

Jay didn't argue. He walked over to Bald Head, cocked his hand all the way back, and came forward with an open hand.

Slapppp!

"Huhh!" Bald Head shouted as he popped into consciousness.

I guess he was taking too long to come all the way back to his senses because Jay slapped the fuck out of him again.

"What the fuck! Nigga, I'll kill you!" Bald Head barked at Jay with his deep voice trying his best to break free of the duct tape wrapped around his body.

Jay stepped out the way as I limped across the kitchen floor. Although I couldn't stand to my full height, I still had my head held high. "Nah, Bald Head. This what's gon' happen. If you don't tell me who sent the hit on me, I'm gon' let these three kill you though and I'm talking about the slow way."

He looked up at me evilly with a bloody face and a big smile like he displayed in the skating rink's bathroom. "It might not be me that does it, but yo' ass gon' die out here, baby girl! Ain't no way around that."

Jay punched him this time. A stiff one to the nose that caused blood to squirt out. "Who the fuck sent you?" Jay asked with his face all up in Bald Head's.

Bald Head hit Jay with a quick, but powerful, headbutt that sent him to the ground with a bloody nose as well. "Aghhhh shit! I'ma kill this fuck nigga!"

Jay was getting up on his feet and I knew he would live up to his words, so I interfered. "I need him alive right now, so chill out."

I looked over at Drama and nodded in Bald Head's direction. He started shaking his head rapidly in disagreement. "Nah, I'm not with the foreplay. That's up Unique's alley. She tortures every side hoe she catch a nigga with. She got plenty of practice," he informed seriously.

I looked at Unique and she shrugged her little shoulders non-chalantly before making her way over towards Bald Head, who was smiling up at her licking his long tongue out to her.

"Ouuuuuueeeee! You probably could do a lot with that tongue huh?" she purred in a soft and seductive voice.

Bald Head nodded his head in agreement while scanning her up and down with his yellowish eyes. "Fuckin' right!"

"What about that dick though?" Unique asked while dropping down onto both knees. She began to massage his penis through the polyester slacks he wore. "Look at you, this muthafucka growing fast. I bet you can work wonders with this too, huh?"

"Man, I'll buss you wide open with this shit in my pants!" he promised.

All the blood from his brain must've been flowing to his dick because he was zoned out. He was locked in on Unique like she was the only person in the room with him.

"I gots to see this shit here," she stated before unbuckling his pants and pulling his dick out.

I looked away at Drama to see his reaction, but this nigga was now sitting on the countertop snacking on a handful of grapes like he wasn't watching his girl with another nigga's dick in her hand.

"Baby, this nigga said he gon' buss me wide open. What you think?" she asked Drama without looking at him. She was too busy stroking Bald Head's dick with her small hands.

Bald Head had his head back in ecstasy, no doubt trying to concentrate on a nut. He was definitely thinking with his little head.

Drama chucked amusingly. "I don't know, shawty. He don't got that curve in his shit like mines. You know how you like them curves."

"Exactlyyyyy! That's definitely right... Looks like I'm going to have to do some construction on this thing here. Pass me one of them steak knives in that rack over there," she requested casually.

Bald Head picked his head up and opened his eyes the wide way. "Holdddd up! Hold up! We ain't even got to do all that. It was Redd, man... Redd the one that's trying to get you whacked. He said something about you sitting on the wrong throne."

Chapter 21

Four hours later, I slowly strolled into Venom's hospital room, but this time the nigga was looking better than me.

He sat up in his bed watching an old episode of *Cheaters* while filing his fingernails. He smiled brightly when he saw me, even brighter than he did before. "If it ain't baby John Wick himself... You look like shit, bruh, but I'm glad you made it out of another jam though. You definitely proving yourself to be solid."

I knew Manny was going to run his mouth. I was already a witness to how fast news could travel around here, so I wasn't surprised that he knew about my run-in from last night. "This shit is really starting to get to me, shawty. I'm not even gon' hold you up. These niggas got me fucked up for real!"

"Calm down! All that extra excitement not gon' help nothing," he schooled while glaring at me seriously. He still hadn't stopped filing his fingernails.

"Man, I'm not you. How am I not supposed to take this shit personally when my *own* fucking kind is trying to kill me? I'm gon' make sure Redd die slow for this shit," I promised seriously. I wasn't a killer and didn't want to become one, but I was willing to handle Redd myself for what he was putting me through.

To my surprise, this nigga Venom starts smiling up at me. "How you figure it out?"

"You knew?" I asked accusingly.

He sat the nail filer down on the dresser and sat back on his bed. "I figured it was him, but I didn't have any proof. That's why I told you to give me some time to figure shit out, but that leads me to this question. Do you have proof? Because those are some strong accusations to be throwing around at a nigga like Redd. That's a whole different breed of nigga right there."

I took my phone out and showed him a video I recorded of Bald Head's confession to being hired by Redd to whack me.

I was about to turn the video off after the confession, but Venom stopped me. "Hold up! I got to see this part too," he said excitedly while watching Jay suffocate Bald Head with a plastic grocery bag. "That lil' nigga got a bright future."

"Yeah, right," I retorted sarcastically. "So, what now? Who I'm supposed to show this to?"

Chapter 22
~ Part 2 ~
Manny

I sat up on the edge of my bed staring into the long mirror that propped up against the wall while listening to Ronte's new hit single that I was featuring on. The song dropped two days ago and already had over two-hundred thousand views on YouTube.

I strolled down all the comments under the video and was blown away by the high amount of good reviews and praise that I was receiving from the fans. It was honestly a bit overwhelming. Everybody was begging for more music from the dude with the wavy hair and the sick flow.

Lately, I had a purpose in life, so it was really hard for me to sleep these days. I haven't got too much sleep since that night I met Rondo at the skating rink almost ten nights ago. My life took a hectic turn once Ronte shouted me out on his Instagram page. It made me an instant celebrity. There were pro's and con's that came with fame, like everything else in life.

"Manny, you got all these niggas posted up in front of my damn apartment and shit. They have been chilling on the stairs across the street for years. Now all of a sudden, they want to kick it on these stairs over here," my whale of a mother informed accusingly, as she walked into my room without knocking.

"I don't got them niggas doing shit! They just want to be close to me since I'm somebody now. You know how that shit goes," I responded after tossing the iPad on my bed, so I could get up and get dressed.

"Yeah, whatever. You could've been a doctor or lawyer. Some shit like that... Musicians just end up strung out on drugs and shell-shocked from all the crazy shit them white devils done did to their asses," she spat before exiting the room without closing the door behind herself.

I just shook my head disappointedly, but I really didn't feel any type of way because she was just being herself. When I came home and shared the good news with her about my newfound fame, she looked me in my eyes with a straight face and told me that I better not sacrifice her for it. That's what I got instead of a congratulations.

She was a naturally negative person, which is why I was moving into my own place tomorrow to get away from her ass.

After I was dressed, I grabbed my oldest son, Trent, and left out of the apartment. When we stepped outside, all eyes were on me.

"If it ain't the Golden Child! 4's up lil' nigga!" Dank greeted as I approached the staircase.

Dank was a heavyset dude in his mid-thirties that's been hustling on the same block for as long as I could remember, but he would never make it off this block because he was one of those niggas that liked to play way harder than he worked.

"All the time... What it's looking like out here?" I asked while pulling my son's hood from inside of his coat, up over his head, to shield him from the chilly breeze that assaulted us all.

Dank shook his head from side-to-side with a sigh. "Man, it's money out here as usual, but it ain't safe bruh."

"Who we beefing with now?" I asked with a raised eyebrow.

"Them boys in blue."

My eyes widened slightly. "The Crips again?"

"Nah, not them. The police, nigga... They just gunned down two Mobsters by the train tracks while chasing them from the store," he informed sadly.

"Damn! They been dropping niggas in public, so I can only imagine how they did them boys behind the scenes," I wondered aloud.

"They did 'em dirty! Stood over them young niggas... Just make sure you be easy out here, lil' nigga. You have shit to lose now," he advised.

Even though I didn't quite trust Dank, I still took his advice. I looked up the street and seen a midnight blue Crown Victoria rolling up on 28" rims. I smiled inwardly because my nigga, Donny, was always right on time.

Donny was the closest thing to a brother I ever had. He was only a year older than me, and we basically had everything in common. But on the outside, we were exact opposites.

I was short, standing at 5'4" and he stood eight inches over me. My skin was light brown like my eyes, but he was dark brown. I had a body full of tattoos, and he only had one on the side of his face. People called us salt-and-pepper behind our backs, but we didn't trip as long as they respected us enough not to say it to our faces.

"Nigga, I heard you before I saw you. You must've got them raggedy-ass speakers fixed?" I asked jokingly after strapping Trent into the backseat and hopping in the front.

He looked over at me with a big smile showing his small shark teeth. "Better know it. Even when we get rich. I'm gon' keep this bitch right here. She got sentimental value."

"Whatever... Just keep that shit down while my son in the car before u burst his eardrums."

He extended his open palm back to the backseat, and Trent gave it a hard slap with a big smile on his face. "So, what's the move?"

"I got to pull up on Nequa first, then we can hand that other business."

117

He nodded his head before hitting a U-turn and rolling up out of my small apartment complex.

Nequa was the one that fronted me my first package of heroin. She'd been holding shit down in our hood years before Dilluminati hit our city, and she was well respected. The fact that she was a woman didn't mean shit. She'd earned her stripes in these streets like everybody else, and she wasn't to be underestimated.

She stayed in a decent house behind my apartment complex, but she was never there. She was always on the move, somewhere else other than her house.

There was this little grass field in our hood where a house should've been, but it was empty. It was a known chill-spot in our hood. She told me to meet her there.

There was a group of Mobsters surrounding her Escalade serving the neighborhood junkies like it was legal. Donny didn't pull onto the field because he didn't want to risk messing up his rims by driving over the curb, so he parked on the street.

I told him to stay in the car with Trent before I hopped out and walked across the field. Niggas showed me extra love as I approached. I flashed a smile, and greeted them back, even though I knew it was fake. These were the same uptight niggas that used to walk past me.

I hopped in the back of the truck with Nequa and was welcomed by a thick cloud of weed smoke. She was dressed nicely kicked back on some boss shit as usual. She held her finger up to make sure I didn't say anything while she was on the phone.

She was talking to her booking agent for an online gambling company. Rumor has it she'd run up a pretty penny gambling with on sports overtime. I set up an account in my sister's name but ended up losing more money than I made, so I just called it quits.

"Alright. It's going down tonight. I got $1,500 on the Grizzlies. If I hit this ticket, that's $6,250!" she informed enthusiastically.

"What's up with you though? How the life of the rich-and-famous treating you?"

I gave her a knowing look. "I'll take famous right about now, but rich? Not yet, big sis'. After I made my investments and fucked with my baby mamas, that lil' $20,000 I got from Ronte was gone."

"That may be the case, but everybody knows you got riches in your future, which is why everybody's acting differently towards you. They all want to get in your favor. I can see that myself, but I can also see a lot of jealousy. You need to watch out," she schooled seriously.

I waved her off dismissively. "You sound like that nigga, Rondo, now. I got everything under control"

"You better take heed, lil' nigga. These streets are grimy, bruh, and niggas will step on you just because they know you about to climb out this shit. I know you ain't got the money right now, but when that shit starts rolling in like it's supposed to, you need to get yo' family and get the fuck up out these trenches!"

I looked her in the eyes and knew that she was genuine. She was one of the few people that actually had my best interest at heart. It was just going to make it even harder to let her down, but not impossible. "I'm sorry to tell you, but I just can't do it. I mean, I understand everything you saying right now, but just like I said in that song with Ronte. I'm not gon' leave this hood until I touch a million. I feel like I got to stand on that shit," I informed matter-a-factly before dapping her up, accepting the package in the brown paper bag that was on her lap, and hopping out of the truck.

I knew she was disappointed in a nigga, but it wasn't for her to understand. Niggas were waiting for me to run up out of the hood so they could talk bad about me, but they had another thing coming. I planned on standing ten toes in the paint.

Chapter 23

"I mean, I feel what she saying, but I definitely understand where you coming from too," Donny stated while cruising smoothly through the hood. "But if we're going to stay in the slums, we gon' have to let somebody in, even if they weren't here from the beginning. I'm gon' handle business, but I'm not an army. We gon' need more muscle."

"We got Slick and Adam with us," I reminded, referring to a pair of niggas our age, who were selling dope for us.

"That's not nearly enough, nigga. Just a couple of young street punks. We need a few OG's behind this shit. We need some muscle, nigga."

I looked out the window while thinking about his statement. I really wasn't trying to embrace these shady ass niggas around here, but it did make sense to let somebody in. It really was the only way. "You right. We'll handle that ASAP."

There were about four sections to our hood. Before Dillumina-ti hit the city, Boonie Doon used to be the hood that never got along with the rest which is what made us close. We're like a big family. Everybody knew everybody, but like most families, everybody was nosey. That's why Donny and I tried to move extra low key since the spotlight was on us.

We pulled up in front of Donny's house towards the middle of the hood and dropped Trent off to play with Donny's little brother. After, we headed to our next destination, but we weren't in the car. We had to travel on foot.

There was a set of woods in the backyard of Donny's house and a path that led through to woods to our destination. There was an opening where an old abandoned tire shop sat.

Two fiends were exiting the building and hit a separate cut that led to a different part of the hood. The patch of woods was at the heart of the hood, and that's why we decided to dust the building off and set up shop there.

We walked inside of the shop, finding Slick, Adam, and two other females chilling on foldable chairs, watching an old horror movie on the flat-screen sitting on the ground. We were still in the process of furnishing the place.

"I know y'all ain't got these hoes up in here!" Donny barked aggressively while peering down at them menacingly.

"Who you calling a hoe, bruh?" Adam asked defensively popping up out of his seat quickly with his chest out.

Unfortunately for him, Donny already had his Glock 19 in his hand. "She a hoe when she in *my* muthafuckin' spot. Especially since we specifically told y'all no niggas and *hoes* allowed. This is a low-key spot, nigga!" Donny reminded with the muzzle of the gun leveled with Adam's forehead.

Adam shot his hands up into the air unconsciously. "Come on bruh! You trippin'!"

"Nah, how the hell I'm tripping? Y'all niggas tripping 'cause y'all ain't following directions. I told y'all niggas that all y'all got to do is follow orders and handle business, and everything was gon' fall in place," said Donny before removing the gun out of his face. "Sit yo' ass down.''

Adam sat back down in his chair. "You got down then. It's all good!" he said through clenched teeth while shaking his head slowly.

"You fuckin' right I got down, nigga! Yo' girl would've never had to see me shine on you if you would've followed directions... It all goes back to what I said before. Follow orders and everything's going to fall in place," Donny promised.

Slick was the smarter one out of him and Adam. Instead of sitting there looking stupid like Adam, he reached down under his chair and grabbed the brown paper bag full of money and tossed it at me.

I opened the bag and peeped inside. It all looked to be there, so I pulled the paper bag I got from Nequa out of my jacket pocket and tossed it to him. "Make that stretch for three days. Fix this place up with the money y'all make off the extra grams," I informed before turning around to exit the shop with Donny on my heels.

Forty minutes later, we were in the parking lot of a plaza on Bragg Boulevard. Donny ate Chinese food while I counted my money in the passenger's seat. We took little pitstops like this all the time, but we stayed on point, which is why we both had our pistols laying on our laps.

We'd just got back into the car. Donny went into the Chinese spot while I hit the Check Cashing place to pick up my money from Western Union. A local rapper from Charlotte, North Carolina sent me $4,400 for me to do a feature on his song for his upcoming mixtape.

"Damn bruh. That's your first feature, and you got $4,400. This shit really getting real," Donny admitted with a smile on his face. I knew he was proud of me for real.

"Real shit, but we can't rely on this shit. Music is a hustle. It'll take too long to run up a million off of rap money, so we got to go hard in the dope game for a few months. Then we can wash that dirty money through Ronte. If Rondo can run up a million in four months by himself, we can do it too." I visioned our near future vividly in my head.

Donny's eyes weren't dreamy like mines. They were down-to-earth. "I don't know about that shit. Four months? Rondo must've dropped the cheat code on you or something?"

"Hell yeah, nigga! Stay focused, spend less, and remain humble," I answered truthfully.

Donny shrugged his shoulders. "I'm following your lead, bruh."

"You know I'm not gon' lead us wrong. We got the key to the game, and we connected now. All we need is that muscle we was talking about and we'll be unstoppable. We guaranteed to make it up out of this shit."

Chapter 24

The Mace brothers were six Muslim brothers who were all down for whatever. From the oldest brother, who was twenty-four, all the way to the youngest brother, who was fifteen. All six of them were about that action. They'd gone to war with entire gangs by themselves.

We chose to pull up on them because they stayed together and didn't really fuck with anybody outside of their family. They were ruthless, but they were loyal, and those were traits that we needed in our soldiers.

Their house was even isolated. They stayed on a very small dead-end street that sat across from a trailer park by itself in an empty lot. They had the perfect spot to operate their drug operation.

Donny associated with Marley. He was the seventeen-year-old middle brother. They did juvenile time together.

Marley was leaning on a 2012 mustard yellow SS Camaro with his oldest brother, Payback. They all looked like different versions of each other. Tall and stocky with sharp facial features. Intimidation was their specialty, and right now, they were doing a good job.

Donny pulled up in front of their house and parked on the curb at the top of the driveway. We hopped out and made our way down the driveway.

"You hit my line talking big business, so I called up the big dawg," Marley informed while tapping Payback on his big arm with his backhand. "He don't like to waste his time, so I'm gon' need for y'all niggas to not make me look stupid today."

I nodded my head understandably. "I had Donny hit your line and we do have big business on the table. This shit really is bigger than business. This YF shit gon' be bigger than life, it's a lifestyle,"

I informed matter-a-factly looking up at them seriously. They towered over my 5'4" frame, but I was going to make them feel my giant voice.

"YF? What the hell is that? What you need from us? I don't get it," Payback fired questions back to back, impatiently.

I pushed my open palms towards the ground motioning for him to take it easy. Donny lit the half-smoked blunt he had behind his ear and passed it to Payback after taking a few puffs himself.

"Yeah, Young & Foolish... Just use yo' head right now, big bruh. You know who I am. I got real-life millionaires behind this shit. If y'all become a part of this shit, y'all gon' have millionaires behind y'all too. The best part about it is that we gon' actually make a difference out here, my nigga. Focus on the youth because they're the future."

Payback had a different look on his face now. It was one of interest. "Oh yeah? Step inside then. Sounds like we need to get comfortable for this talk right here." He led the way down the driveway towards the house.

As I followed him down the driveway, I saluted myself for another victory. Everything was falling in place like dominoes.

Later on that evening, the sun had just disappeared, but my night was still kind of young. Right now, I was at Trent's mother's house sitting on the floor with my back against the wall. I was continuously recounting my money even though I knew exactly how much I had. I was playing mind games with her ass. We had a fucked-up history and we were very toxic for each other, but we kept it cordial for the sake of the kids.

When I met her four years ago, I lied about my age and she didn't find out my real age until after we had Trent. She got mad and ended things between us after that. She fucked up when she tried to keep me away from my son, so I had my sister, Jelissa, hop on her ass to convince her otherwise.

Lately, she'd been acting all high maintenance since she was pregnant by one of them scamming niggas in Tadoe's camp, but now it was my turn to shit on her ass.

"You don't got to have that big ass gun out like that. You do have a whole son right there watching you," said Niecey, referring to my Mac-11 I had on the floor next to me.

"It's gon' be the same shit when I got him with me at my video shoots and shit. My whole life revolves around money and guns now," I retorted without giving her the benefit of eye contact.

"You got to do better," Dasia, her best friend, added sitting on the couch next to her. I didn't know if she was talking to me or Niecey.

I finally looked up. "That's coming from the same girl whose baby daddy left her for a bitch with one leg... No, you got to do better. My future real bright. I'm doing just fine. Ain't that right, Trent?"

"Damn right!" he answered in his little voice proudly.

Niecey cringed at me. "I told you about teaching my son that bullshit! You so damn ignorant, I swear!"

"Nah, I got plenty of sense. My recent accomplishments is showing that. I just like to get up under yo' bougie ass skin." I stuffed my money into my pant pocket and my Mac into my MCM book bag before standing. "Let me get up out of here before your lil' boyfriend pulls up and gets the wrong idea. I just came to drop my lil' nigga off. I'll be back soon, but I got places to be right now."

I kissed Trent on the forehead and exited the house despite his cries for me to stay. I knew Niecey's gold-digging ass probably wanted me to stay too, but I wasn't willing to let her too close. She wasn't the loyal type and that's not what I needed around me, so I had to keep her at a distance.

She was my son's mother, so I would eventually put her in a position to be somebody in life, but for now, she just had to sit on the bench until I was ready to put her in the game.

Chapter 25

A little past midnight, I sat in a downtown studio with Donny and my new producer. I had just finished the verse on the song I was paid for. It was the easiest $4,400 I ever made in my life. I could definitely get used to this.

The producer was at his desk fooling with my voice on his computer screens while Donny and I sat on a sofa in the lounge area smoking our lungs out. These were the times I came up with my best ideas. When I was tired and high.

"I was thinking. Since we stressing that we all for the youth, why not make a children's clothing line out of this shit. It don't got to stop there. We can open a few programs, fix up that old gym on Bragg Boulevard for them, and all," I envisioned out loud.

Donny sat up and looked over at me. "I mean, that sound like some shit Jay-Z would put together. You really think it could be done for real? Sound like a lot of work."

"Of course. I'm plugged in like a socket now. It won't be too hard to get anything done, to be honest. It's all just one phone call away. I just don't want to be the average rapper out here. I'm really trying to use this fame and money for good, bruh. What you think?" I asked even though I knew Donny would go along with me regardless. I still asked for his opinion to make him feel appreciated.

"Shit, to be honest, I would've never come up with no shit like that... You really need to leave these streets alone, bruh. You got so much more going for yourself. Not many people get chances like you. You don't want to fuck that up playing in these streets when you don't got to," he philosophized seriously.

I waved him off. "Just chill, I just need you to make sure a nigga don't kill me. Everything gon' be straight. Just a four-month run and I'm out."

"Fuck it. Let's do it! I got faith in this shit my nigga. I'm trying to make it to the big leagues." Now, his eyes were dreamy. He had a vision.

"Watch us turn them dreams into reality," I agreed passionately.

The positive energy in the room was so strong that I could almost taste it. Great things were in the making. Every day of our lives was now history in the making.

***

The next morning, Jelissa woke me up energetically. "Bruh! Get the fuck up! Today is that day!"

I literally just closed my eyes not even a whole two hours ago. I was *very* tired and aggravated, but today was a special day and I had a lot to do. For the next four months, it was all gas and no brakes.

I popped my eyes open and looked at her standing over me in a stylish pantsuit. She looked good. "Damn sis', you used that money I gave you wisely, huh?"

"I did good, huh?" she asked while performing a slow Cinderella three-sixty spin. "If I'm going to be a realtor, I have to look the part."

I wasn't even groggy anymore; her energy was coming off of me. "Exactly! That's my muthafuckin' sister! Can't have you working at nobody's Post Office. Our bloodline is royal now, so we got to carry ourselves like it."

I could tell the life that I was speaking into her was filling her up because she was standing proudly with her head up for a change. Although Jelissa was beautiful, she always suffered from insecurities since she was young. "I like that."

I sat up in my bed and released a long yawn when my sons came running into the room recklessly. Ronny, the older one, was chasing, Junie, the youngest one. These two stayed with me most of the time because their mother, Destiny, decided she wanted to serve the country with the Army instead of raising her damn kids.

"Daddy! Junie slapped me in the face," Ronny informed heatedly as a laughing, Junie, ran in between the safety of my legs.

"You slapped yo' big brother?" I asked looking down at Junie's little badass.

"No! He-he lying!"

Ronny built up enough balls to charge at Junie, but Jelissa picked him up before he could get to Junie. "Let me take him to get dressed while you handle Junie," she offered playfully despite Ronny's cries for revenge.

I was so grateful for Jelissa. She helped me raise them from day one. I owed her the world.

The real estate meeting went well. With my $8,500 and Jelissa's good credit, we walked away with a house in a decent neighborhood. There was a sizable amount of work that needed to be done before we could put it up for renovation, but it was still a big step for us.

We also invested another few thousand dollars on four months' rent for a decent double-wide trailer right off of Bragg Boulevard a few minutes away from my hood. It was in a mobile park nicknamed The Chase. It was a temporary arrangement and it was worth every penny to get us up out of my mother's apartment. Sadly, she was like poison to our growth, so Jelissa and I made the better choice for us.

While Jelissa showed the boys their new playhouse, I stood on the porch smoking a joint while scanning the area carefully. I didn't trust these niggas out here, so I had my Glock tucked in my left armpit for easy access. It wasn't a huge trailer park, but it wasn't small either. I knew all about The Chase and even knew a few people out here, but there was still a lot of people I didn't know.

A group of four niggas, and one female, were walking down the street looking my way, and I looked right back at their asses trying to recognize one of them.

I usually kept on hood gear when I ran the streets, but today was special and I was dressed for the part. I had on a pair of white Christian Louboutin, Gucci jeans to match, and a dark grey Burberry button-down shirt under a grey pea coat to match. My chain and the grey tented Cartier lenses I wore on my face completed the outfit.

"I know that ain't that boy, Manny! What you doing out here, bruh? Where you been?" a skinny dread headed boy asked while walking across the street towards the stairs of my porch.

I recognized him as he neared. His name was Antonio. We went to school together. I hadn't seen him since my last day at school last semester before I dropped out.

"I've been handling business. Got a lot of shit in the works... What's up with you?" I asked as he climbed the stairs.

His associates kept their distance on the street, but they were all peering at me with recognition. "Mannnn! This shit hard for a young nigga these days. I'm not even gon' lie."

"That's a shame on yo' big homies, and I'm not even talking about them giving you a hand-out. A big homie is supposed to give all they lil' homies the game so they can make their own way. What's up with that? If I'm not mistaken, you're supposed to have a baby on the way. Ain't no way you supposed to be walking around here broke."

He wasn't surprised by my bluntness; I was known to speak my mind. "The original OG's went to prison, and the niggas that's running shit now don't show no love to the young niggas out here."

"Do y'all have $4,000 between y'all right now?" I asked seriously, loud enough for the other ones to hear.

He hesitated at first, but did some recovering after a few seconds. "Hell nah. I'm not even gon' lie. When I say it's ugly, that's what I mean."

"And when I say the grass is greener on the other side, that's what I mean."

Chapter 26

Later that afternoon, Donny and I were on the road on the way to Rondo's house.

"Chase Gang! Really bruh?" Donny asked disappointedly with his hands gripped on the steering wheel. He definitely wasn't a yes-man. If he didn't agree with anyone, he would let them know. I was no exception. "It's already bad enough you moved out there, but now you trying to recruit the whole hood? That's crazy! You the same nigga that just said he's not trying to embrace all these niggas."

I chuckled lightly. "Not the whole hood, just the young niggas for now. I did say that, but you're right. We need to expand. Why not Chase Gang? Them niggas got potential."

"I don't know about that one. We know a couple of them niggas from school, but I still don't trust it."

"They're not stupid enough to try nothing crazy... Them niggas just want a plug. They want a chance, so why not? I got a good feeling about it. Especially if I put Antonio in charge over the section. He got a lil' influence out there already and it's just gon' grow when I give him everything that he needs to brainwash them niggas," I explained as we pulled up into Rondo's outer driveway.

Donny parked at the head of the driveway that was connected to Rondo's house. "I hope it don't, but if shit goes sour with them niggas, I'm gon' tell you that *I told you so*," he promised.

"Stay positive my nigga," I advised before getting out of his car and leading the way to Rondo's front door.

I hadn't seen Rondo face-to-face since that night at the skating rink. It was definitely a night to remember. He was another hot topic around the city, and the two failed attempts on his life only intensified his legend. Now, he was labeled a made-man in our eyes around the city. He'd earned his stripes.

He tried to get me to meet with him yesterday, but I was busy, so I told him I'd pull up on him today. Jay had opened the door for us, and lead me to Rondo, who was in the bed fooling around with stocks on his phone. Donny stayed downstairs with Jay and Rondo's other two shooters.

"I been talking to Venom, Venom been talking to Prima, Prima been talking to her friends, her friends been talking to the streets, and the streets say you been a busy man out there," Rondo said evenly while giving me this look. It was like a kind of look a father gave his son when he was studying him.

"Yeah, I have been really busy. I'm trying to do what you did, big bruh. I'm trying to run up a million dollars in four months," I informed confidently. "You gave me the recipe and I'm about to run with that shit."

He adjusted himself in the bed with a slight smile on his face. "You making it sound like it's easy or something."

"Nah, I never said it would be easy. I know better than that, but I do have faith I'm myself. You and Ronte already gave me all the tools I need, now all that's left for me to do is get to work and build this empire." I countered before passing him the blunt of weed that I already had pre-rolled before I came in.

He declined while shaking his head from side-to-side. "Nah, I'm good. I got to keep a clear head right now. Too much going on."

"Yeah, I probably wouldn't be smoking if I was you either… Word on the streets is that yo' old Don that sent you up here is still trying to get you whacked," I informed while watching for his reaction.

To my surprise, he laughed. "Just focus on yourself, and your mission. I'll be straight." He pointed over at the walk-in closet. I could see inside because the door was open.

"What?" I asked with my head turned in that direction.

"Go in there and grab the red gym bag on the floor," he instructed before picking his phone back up after it vibrated.

My anxiousness to see what was in the bag caused me to get up faster than I wanted to. I went inside the closet, picked the bag up, carried back over the Rondo, and dropped it on the bed.

Rondo sat his phone back down, unzipped the bag, and took two stacks of money out. "I'm gon' match that $20,000 Ronte gave you, but you need to make this shit count. I already told you, but I feel like you need to hear it again... Your success is vital to the rebirth of this city. This is my vision, but those are your people. Even though you're young, they'll be more comfortable following you than an outsider. Use your money and influence for good. Make a difference out there and be the Neighborhood Hero they need, shawty."

The weed had me higher than Giraffe's pussy, but I was paying close attention to his words and digesting them deep down. "Ain't no hope for Fayetteville no more. They too far gone, that's why I'm gon' create a new world for them. I'm gon' take 'em to Rondoville!" I promised after accepting the stacks of blue faced hundreds from him.

Malik D. Rice

Chapter 27

"I fuck with that nigga, Jay. He like a crazier version of me. He cool, but it's not hard to tell that nigga got demons." Donny admitted while cruising through traffic on the way to our next destination.

I was on the passenger's seat thumbing through my money. It felt so good to me. I used to dream about counting this type of money.

"Nah, fuck Jay. Them other two got a wicked ass look in their eyes. I can't even hold eye-contact with them folks. Shit creepy as fuck." I spat seriously.

Donny nodded his head in agreement. "Yeah, it is something about them." He glanced over at me. "Why Rondo didn't just give you the drugs instead? He know you gon' flip that money."

"Him, and Ronte don't want me in the streets, so they just give me the money instead of the drugs to make them feel better, I guess. I really don't give a damn because neither one of them niggas was obligated to give me *shit*, so I'm grateful dawg."

We made a left turn into the parking lot of Cross Creek Mall. Christmas eve was tomorrow, and I still hadn't done any shopping. I'd been too busy, so I had to grab a few last-minute gifts for my sons, but everybody else would get cash instead.

For some reason, Donny, parked a little way away from the entrance of the mall, so we ended up taking a stroll.

"Yoooo, Donny!" Someone shouted aggressively startling both me, and Donny.

We were so high, and paranoid, that we both spun around and drew our pistols off our hips in the same motion, ready to eliminate the potential oncoming threat.

"Woahhhhhh! It's me y'all! It's Gino, just chill!" He yelled with his hands up.

After we put the face with the name, we quickly tucked our pistols before someone saw them. Gino was an associate of Donny's, but he never stayed around too long because he stayed in-and-out of jail.

He looked like he was twenty-seven with his height, weight, and beard.

"Oh, shit! What's going on nigga? Where the hell you been?" asked Donny as Gino caught up to us.

"You know I just got out the county a few weeks ago. I'm on prohibition right now. I got to slow down because a nigga 17 now, and they starting to charge a nigga as an adult."

Donny looked him up-and-down. "You looking good for your-self out here nigga. Who you done robbed this time?" Donny asked half-jokingly, half seriously.

"Nobody that didn't deserve it" Gino retorted unapologetically, then looked my way. "Lil' Manny. You done beat the odds, and I'm proud of you, nigga. If you ever need some work put in, let me know. I got a lil' pack of wolves that's gon' slide when I say so!"

I nodded my head in understanding. "I'll keep that in mind, but right now, we got a tight schedule, so I'll have Donny hit you if we ever need you," I informed dismissively before pounding Gino's hand and walking off towards the mall.

Donny did the same before catching up with me. "Why the hell you brush him off like that?"

"Because I don't trust the nigga, and you shouldn't either. I keep telling yo' ass that," I advised seriously. "Especially now! Nigga, he know you my right-hand-man, so he'll try to play up under you just to get in the yard... I don't need no snakes in my grass bruh."

Donny didn't even respond. He just kept walking, so I left it alone. I didn't need a response, as long as he listened**

The mall was packed for a Thursday, but it was only because of the holiday. My first stop was to the toy store. It was jam packed, but I would wait in any line to get my sons some toys for Christmas.

I was in the store, talking to Donny about a Nerf gun that I wanted to buy Trent, when I heard a woman call my name out excitedly. "Mannnyyyyy! That is you, boy! Should've known you was going to have Donny's bad self with you! Y'all remember me?" A short red headed teenage girl asked standing next to an older version of herself. Had to be her mother.

It took a few seconds, after I turned around, for me to finally recognize her. She went to elementary school with us, but we never seen her after fifth grade.

"Yeah, I think I remember you. What 'bout you Manny?" asked Donny curiously.

I nodded my head up-and-down slowly with a smirk. "Yeahhh. Lil' Taliyah. How could I forget?"

That put a big bright smile on her dark skin face. "Awwww, that's so cute! Anyway, I'm heading out of here. Just came to grab a few toys for my little cousin, but I'm definitely glad I ran into you. I'm not going to hold your shopping up, just make sure you keep doing what you're doing. You have a lot of potential, and I can see you doing great things, just *pleaseeee* don't let these dudes kill you out here, and I'm referring to dudes in the street and the police... Keep him safe Donny!" She was already walking off as she said that last sentence.

I stood there watching her walking off, both, admiring her backside, and digesting the words she just dropped on me. She definitely had just said a mouthful, and it was hitting me. Somehow, coming from her, it made me look at things different.

"Pleaseeee don't let these dudes kill you out here." Those words would definitely stick with me.

Chapter 28

"Everybody want to know about me, and where I'm from. Well, this a letter to the world. My name is DG Manny, and I'm from Rondoville...

Told my sista we straight!
Put the food on the plate!
So, you know that a young nigga pavin' the wayyy!
He ain't talkn' 'bout money!
He ain't talkin' 'bout nothin'!
You know that a nigga on a paper chaseee!"

My voice flowed out rapidly through the speakers as my new single *Rondoville* played in Trappa's living room.

Nequa had texted me while I was at the mall, trying to meet with me, but I let her know I was busy at the time, so we set up a time to meet later that night at eleven.

Since I didn't have a car at the moment, she picked me up at my spot in The Chase. From there, she drove over to Shaw Road to Ridge Park where Trappa was waiting on us.

"Everybody was talking about this song yesterday when it dropped, so I went and checked it out... It's a nice ass song, but I couldn't enjoy it no matter how many times I played it over. I wasn't focused." Trappa informed from the other side of the living room sitting on the arm of the couch by the front door.

"What you talkin' about?" I asked then stated with a twisted face.

He turned the music down with the remote that was in his hand. "We from the place where dreams like yours don't come true lil' nigga. Everybody out here calling you the chosen one. You supposed to be the one to put *Fayetteville* on the map...

That's why I couldn't enjoy the song because the whole time I been trying to figure out what the fuck is a Rondoville!"

The agitation in his voice was real, but he kept his cool. "If you really look at it, Rondo is the best thing that ever happened to this city. The real definition of a Neighborhood Hero. If it wasn't for him, none of this shit would be possible. It's gon' be a real change around here. Watch."

Trappa shot Nequa a disapproving glance and shot me an even worse one. "I understand what the nigga did for you, but I'm not telling you this for me, I'm telling you this for your own good... Take that song down and fix that Rondoville shit. Redd not happy about that shit lil' bruh. You're basically the face of the whole city to the world right now, which mean you a politician. He can't have you going around giving Rondo glory over this city."

I looked at Nequa right in the eyes and shook my head. "Not you too big sis'! Redd is in jail with all types of charges, and Rondo is out here trying to make our city a better place. Redd only give a fuck about himself. It shouldn't be hard to choose! Redd is irrelevant right about now, honestly."

Trappa stood up while looking at Nequa, and waved my way dramatically, basically telling her to talk some sense into me.

She scooted up on the edge of the couch returning my eye contact. "Look, Manny... You know I won't tell you nothing wrong. I might not have the biggest heart around here, but you know I always favored you. I knew it was something about you all this time. You know I fuck with you, so listen to me when I tell you that that nigga Redd is a lot more relevant than you think. He in that jail cell pulling more strings than ever. They fucked up when they locked him up because they just gave the nigga more time to think."

It amazed me how Redd still held fear over them even when he wasn't actually there. He was a powerful, and manipulative, man that was capable of a lot, but Rondo was powerful too, and that's who I owed my loyalty to... my Don. "Like I said, I'm not worried about Redd. He was the king of Fayetteville, and that place brought nothing but pain. Rondo came and created his own world... Rondoville."

"You a big dawg now, huh? Hope you build to last lil' nigga. You know how cheap life can be in this here jungle. You see the hard time Rondo having? He barely hanging on by a string out here. How much longer you think he gon' last? Matter-a-fact, how much longer you think Venom gon' last? Use your head lil' nigga. You trying to save a city that don't want to be saved. You just got to survive out here." Trappa countered grimly.

I smiled at his indirect threats. "I mean, I just seen Rondo today, and my nigga standing *tall*. You tripping, and when it comes to me, I guess we just gon' have to see huh?" I never said anything about Venom because that scared me, and if I spoke on him, I was scared fear would show in my eyes.

"Wait, so let me get this straight... Redd behind all this shit that been going on?" Donny asked while pacing back-and-forth, on the walkway, in front of me.

I was sitting on the steps of his house catching him up to speed on the meeting I had with Trappa last night. "I'm talking about *everything* nigga! Rondo, Venom, niggas getting robbed, and all that shit."

A cold breeze brushed past us, causing Donny to stop in his tracks, and shiver. He only had on an Adidas track suit. "I still don't get it."

"I didn't get it at first either, but now I got a better understanding after Trappa's stupid ass put me all the way on game last night." I zipped my True Religion coat up and pulled my matching skull cap down over my ears. "This was supposed to be a suicide mission for Rondo all along. It's basically designed for him to lose out here, so that's why he got me. He need me just as much as I need him. That's why I'm so important."

"Keep going," he instructed with a roll of his hand.

"Redd was supposed to whack Rondo, so Swagg would have a choice but to make Trappa the Don. That's right up Redd's alley since he got Trappa wrapped around his finger, but the shit harder than he expected. And he probably feel like he can't trust Venom since he embraced Rondo, or some shit... I don't know the whole story, but I do know this shit deeper than the surface, and it's a whole war going on behind the scenes."

He walked over to the stairs and popped-a-squat next to me. "So, what's the plan? We don't even know who all Redd got his claws in. What if he end up with a spy in our circle?"

"I guess we just going to have to play our cards close and test the niggas close to us for now. I got a feeling shit about to get hectic. We can't let these niggas kill me, bruh."

Chapter 29

A few hours later, I had let my son's open up a few of their Christmas gifts up under the tree for Christmas Eve while I stood next to, Jelissa, who sat on the high stool leaning on the wooden kitchen counter looking at me sideways. "So, you really not going to tell me what's going on? We supposed to be best friends, Manny! That's lame as hell!"

I could tell she really felt some type of way for real, but I didn't want her to worry, so I played my cards close with her as well. "You is my best friend, girl. It's just better that you don't know no details right now, trust me! You just said yesterday that you got faith in me, right?"

She nodded her head reluctantly.

"Alright then. If you really had faith in me, you would follow my lead without question. I'm young, but you know I got a brain. I'm smart enough to make this shit happen for real... I just need y'all secure, so I can focus on my mission." I leaned on the counter. "Tomorrow I got Santa coming to help them open they presents, and the next day, you need to start packing y'all shit up."

"Make up your mind, Manny. You done showed the boys their own rooms, and they seem like they like the place." She reasoned.

"Listen, fuck this trailer! I'm gon' put y'all somewhere way better than this. Just start packing like I said." I was trying to remain patient with her.

Her eyes rolled in her head. "What about your birthday? How you know I didn't have nothing planned for you?

"God damn, Lissa! Fuck my birthday man! Just do what the fuck I'm telling you to do bruh!" I snapped and regretted it instantly.

"How you gon' get mad at me for worried about yo' stankin' ass! Let me find out that money fucking your head up already...

You better not prove mama right. I'm gon' follow your lead because I do believe in you, but you better not self-destruct out here." She warned before getting up and storming off towards her room.

I took a deep breath while looking at my sons playing with their toys joyfully. They depended on me. A lot of people were depending on me, and the pressure was applied. I felt it weighting on my soul already. The goal was not to let it crush me. I had to remain solid.

That night, I found myself back inside of Rondo's house, but this time we held our meeting in the kitchen. I requested to meet him on an urgent note, and he invited me over for dinner. I rented a car from a crack smoker in The Chase, for a couple of 20's, and made my way there.

Malika prepared a nice soul food meal with Unique's help. Everybody else ate in the living room, while me and Rondo dined at the kitchen tablet for privacy.

"Now, you can tell me what's so important." Rondo informed with a mouth full of cheese macaroni. "Look like you got a lot on yo' mind right about now."

"Matter-a-fact, I do... I finally know why you smirked at me like that when suggested that your old Don was trying to whack you. You knew it was Redd all along." I accused sternly with a straight face.

He nodded his head slowly in agreement. "Yeah, I did know, but so what? I'm not obligated to share everything with you. It don't concern you. This between me and Redd."

"Noooooo! It's way bigger than you and him. I know about Venom too."

That seemed to get his attention because he dropped his fork. "You been talking to that nigga?" he asked with a flared nose, and a heated gaze.

"Nah, I been talking to yo' boy, Trappa, who might as well be the niggas eyes and ears."

He laughed. "That nigga days is in the double digits right about now. He won't last too long."

"That's funny because he said the *same* shit about yo' ass, but I defended you. You know why? Because that's what family do. When you did what you did for me, I started looking at you like family. We on the same team, and I chose sides nigga, so you might want to think about that the next time you feel like you want to hold some useful information away from me." It was vital for me and Rondo to get on the same page.

He sat back in his chair studying me while playing with his gold teeth with his tongue. That lasted for a few slow seconds before he spoke again. "So, Redd tried to have you whacked too?" The heat was back in his gaze at the thought.

I shook my head side-to-side rapidly. "Not yet... He really mad at me because of that whole Rondoville shit, and Trappa told me all I had to do was change it, and I was gon' be good, but I basically said fuck him."

"Damn! That definitely wasn't part of the plan."

I shrugged. "Shit happens, and we just got to deal with it when it do. I'm not gon' let that nigga intimidate me. I know we got what it take to beat him, I just need you all the way behind me bruh. This YF shit gon' be the answer to all our problems... But first, I need a favor from you."

He motioned for me to continue with a slight nod.

"I need a spot out of town for my folks to stay. At least for four months. Shit should be smooth by then." I explained carefully.

Rondo smiled to my surprise. "Family is important, and I respect that request right there. Tells me *a lot* about you... Don't worry, I know just the place."

Malik D. Rice

Chapter 30
Two Weeks Later

It made sense for Donny to move into the trailer with me after Jelissa and the boys left. Rondo kept his word by finding a house in Atlanta where they could stay. I tried getting Niecey to take Trent down there too, but she wasn't trying to hear it. I didn't even attempt to approach my other baby mother. That lil' bitch was the devil. She never let me see my son, but I had something planned for her ass too.

I sat up on my bed bobbing my head to a new beat my producer had just sent me. I was mumbling random lyrics, trying to find the right delivery I wanted to use for the song.

Knock! Knock!

Someone was at my door.

"Come in!" I instructed.

Donny walked in my room with a weird look on his face.

"What?" I asked impatiently, thinking something serious had just happened.

"That shit smell different. You got a different strand of weed you been holding out on?" he asked with a growing smile.

"Yeah, Rondo dropped this off last night. Shit smoking," I admitted with my arm extended passing him the joint.

He accepted. "Aye, on some real shit though, how long you planning on saying holed up in this muthafucka? You ain't stepped foot outside of this trailer in a week, bruh. Can't have niggas thinking we hiding scared and shit."

"Niggas gon' think what they want and say what they want, but they gon' stay right there where they at. Instead of worrying about them, they spending their time worrying about us... Redd sitting in that cell using all that time to mastermind the game. He ain't gon' be the only one." I couldn't help but picture Redd in that jail cell pacing back-and-forth perfecting the plot on my death.

"Aight. I understand all that, but you been in the spot for a week workin' like a fuckin' dog. Let's go enjoy the night, bruh. We pulled in eighty thousand this week, nigga! We doing *numbers* out here, I think we deserve a night out."

I sighed slightly. "If I do go, we gon' have to take a couple of the Mace brothers with us. I'm not taking no chances out here... Where the hell you trying to go anyway?"

He was fumbling with one of his new YF chains as a slow smile appeared on his narrow face. "Just chill! You gon' thank me later."

After Ronte posted me on his Instagram page, he explained to me the importance of fame. It was rare, so I couldn't be just posting anybody on my page, but Donny wasn't anybody. He was my right-hand-man, so I posted him on my page, giving him a name all for himself.

I'd mentioned him in the song I did with Ronte and on my new single. People were familiar with the young hoodlum. Some of the celebrities from my page followed him as well and that's how we ended up backstage at an R&B concert in Greensboro, North Carolina.

Apparently, Donny had been secretly building a bond with a sixteen-year-old girl named Hennessey. She was the baby sister of Princess Demy, a fast and upcoming R&B superstar who'd just signed a major recording deal with Epic Records about six months ago.

I watched Donny hit Hennessey with his signature talk game. Hennessey sat on his lap while he sat on a chair whispering sweet shit into her ear. I couldn't suppress the oncoming smile on my face if I wanted to.

"You over here cheesing and shit like you know something I don't. How long you think it's going to take him to hurt my lil' sister?" Demy asked in a soft voice after taking a seat on the leather couch next to me.

I must've really been focused on Donny and Hennessey because I didn't even see her approach the couch. I didn't have any plans on saying a word to her because I didn't want to seem like a groupie, but the fact that she approached me was alright by me. I still played it cool.

She probably thought that I was looking at her with a blank face, but I was just higher than a space shuttle. The fact that she was drop-dead gorgeous didn't help either. I was kind of frozen by her beauty. I just gazed at her intensely, admiring her neatly placed baby hairs and her golden-brown skin that was covered with glittered lotion. She looked like a real princess with her expensive ballgown and tiara on her head.

"You rudely ignored my stylist when she approached you and that was understandable because you big time and all. Maybe she wasn't worthy of your attention, but you talking to royalty now, baby, so I'm gon' need you to act like it," she snapped sassily with a lot of neck movement.

My smile was returning. I loved the Louisiana accent mixed with her voice. She was definitely a winning prize. The fact that she was on my case about not giving her enough of my attention did wonders to my ego!

"My bad, baby girl. Don't take it like that, I was just admiring yo' beauty... And to answer yo' question, that depends on her. Donny is a real enforcer by nature. As long as she's submissive, she shouldn't have a problem," I informed matter-a-factly real smooth-like.

She nodded her head slowly. "She's definitely that. That's just my baby sister and I want to make sure she's secure. I don't know what that nigga be telling her, but he got Hennessey fucked up already."

"I'm not surprised," I responded in the midst of laughter.

Demy's road manager walked up to inform her that she was expected on stage in five minutes.

"Let me go turn these folks up real quick," she boasted confidently. "Maybe you can smoke some of that good shit with me after I'm done. I'm trying to get on whatever cloud you on because you look high as hell," she joked while flashing that big white smile of hers.

I licked my lips seductively. "It'll be my pleasure."

Chapter 31

The next morning, I had an early meeting with Nequa at my spot. I would usually meet her wherever she named, but shit was quickly changing. I was basically a made-man myself, and people were treating me accordingly.

After that night at Trappa's spot, Rondo made it clear that I didn't have to answer to *anyone* but him and Ronte. The Young & Foolish brand was growing, and more people were hopping on the bandwagon as the days passed. Donny and I had a lot on our plates.

I knew Nequa was on the enemy's side and I hadn't said a word to her since she dropped me off that night. She knew why. That's why when she called me, she basically begged for me to meet with her.

I purposely flexed my muscle by summoning a healthy amount of my soldiers to be present for the meeting. Antonio and basically every young nigga from The Chase posted up outside around my trailer, while Payback and Marley kicked it in the living room with me. Donny never came back with me last night. He was spending the rest of the weekend holed up in a hotel with Hennessey.

I was chopping it up with Payback about my current situation.

"For you to be your age and accomplishing the shit you doing is a blessing. Ain't no doubt about that, but you got to try *hard* to make sure you don't let your head blow up to the point where you feel like you got it all figured out. That's when you go downhill because you'll never know everything, so life will always be a learning process," he schooled in his usual serious tone.

I fucked with Payback and planned to keep him close. He had a head on his shoulders, and he was a different type of nigga. Although I was basically over him in rank, I still looked up to him the same as Rondo and Ronte. That's why I recruited the Mace brothers in the first place. They were another breed.

"That's some real shit too, big bruh. I'm gon' keep that in mind too because it definitely has been hard for a nigga to stay grounded. All this money and fame make it *real* hard!" I admitted truthfully.

"Exactly... Keep that in mind when Nequa shows up."

Fifteen minutes later, Nequa was sitting across from me at my kitchen table. "I see you got yo' own lil' army now. That's wassup," she observed out loud after taking a look back at Payback and Marley.

"Straight like that. It's definitely a wise decision, but you know why though," I countered holding eye contact with her.

It was weird because this was a lady that I looked up to like a big sister. I once trusted her with my life, now she was a whole enemy. Just that fast.

"How you plan on winning this lil' war?" she asked seriously. But she couldn't be serious.

"I mean, that's something I would normally discuss with people on my side of the field." I kept my tone and temper low, even though I felt like she was here playing mind games with me. It could've been my paranoia, so I just went with the flow.

"Listen. I done talked to Rondo personally. I know he's for the betterment and he got you on the same shit. He knew what he was going when he put you on... Now that I see you got the potential to go toe to toe with a monster like Redd, I want to help you beat him. That nigga done brought too much pain and agony to this city."

I sat there with an even face while I digested her words. "And how do I know Redd didn't send you? I honestly don't trust shit right now."

"I knew you was gon' say that, so I'm gon' drop some useful information on you... Find somebody to take out Dizzy. He the one doing most of Redd's dirty work! Who you think keep gunning at Venom?"

***

"I understand that y'all niggas are paranoid and want to play y'all cards close, but I'm gon' need y'all to understand that I'm on y'all muthafuckin' side, man!" I spat firmly while pacing the floor in Venom's hospital room.

Venom sat up in his bed while Rondo leaned back on the wall with his foot up. They both were looking at me and quietly listening to me vent.

"I'm wrapped up in this shit too, you know! Redd wants to take my head off too, you know!" I barked matter-a-factly.

"Calm the fuck down jit! You doing a good job for a lil' nigga yo' age. I honestly thought Rondo was trippin' when he told me about you, but I see he was onto something," Venom stated in the same manner. "Rondo didn't tell you about Dizzy because I told him not to. I'm gon' handle that issue personally... All you got to do is keep rapping how you rapping, and don't let them fuck niggas kill you."

Malik D. Rice

Chapter 32

"Here! That's for the month right there." My mother placed a small wad of money on her dining room table where I sat eating leftover spaghetti she'd made. "Didn't nobody tell you to pay my bills up for six months. When I say I want no parts of that evil money, I mean directly *and* indirectly! I really don't want you in my house, but I tolerate your presence. I won't tolerate that evil money though, so stop trying lil' boy!"

I looked down at the money on the table and back up at her with an open mouth full of food. "What's wrong with you?"

"Me? Ain't shit wrong with me! I've been this way since before you were born, boy! What's wrong with you? You the one that got bodyguards standing in front of my house acting all high-maintenance and shit!" She peered down at me in disgust.

Clang!

I dropped my fork onto my plate. "Why you can't just be happy for a nigga, ma? You negative as hell! Just because you've been stuck in your ways forever, don't mean it's the right way... This might be evil money, so I can't say nothing about that, but guess what? I'm out here doing really good things with it!" I loved my mother and was trying my best to include her as a part of my life, but she was making it *very* difficult.

I could tell by the look in her eyes she was about to snap. I don't even know why I even bothered to speak sense into her. "Get the fuck up out of my house right now! How dare you come up in here talking all disrespectful to me?"

"Ma, you always say that when Jelissa or I tell you some real shit about yourself," I added more fuel to the fire unconsciously.

She snapped her neck back with an open mouth. "Don't worry about it. Stay yo' lil' smart ass right there... Got something for yo' ass!" she mumbled the last part as she stormed down the hall towards her bedroom.

I knew she was going to grab her wooden bat and I definitely didn't want those problems, so I quickly got up and left.

"You good?" Payback asked me after seeing how fast I left out of the door. He posted up outside the apartment with Marley while I was inside.

"Yeah, man. She just tripping," I answered before leading the way to my new Escalade in the parking lot.

"Yoooo, Manny! Let me holla at you for a lil' bit!" Dank hollered from across the street.

After I moved from the hood, he took his flunkies and set up shop back in the original spot. I knew my mother was happy about that much.

I told Payback and Marley to wait for me in the truck while I went to holler at Dank. I had my Glock with a 30-round clip if he tried anything stupid, but I doubted it. "Wassup?" I asked dryly.

"Look. I'm the one that told Nequa to go make shit right with you. I was like, *that lil' nigga on the winning team. We might as well fuck with him since he from the hood, even though he don't stay in the hood...* Just show the hood love, how you show out there in The Chase." He rubbed his hands together in a prayer position trying to warm them against the cold weather.

I nodded my head approvingly, even though I knew the nigga was lying. He knew that I knew he was lying, but I just played along. He really just wanted to be seen having a private conversation with me, so he could go back and lie to his flunkies about what we were talking about. I knew him all too well.

"You know I will. That was good lookin' out for putting a good word in for me with Nequa. I didn't want to be beefing with my own hood, but check this out. I got a few things I need to check out, so I'm gon' have to jet my nigga. I'm gon' catch you later," I said before shaking his hand and rushing back to my truck, to evade the sharp cold winds.

Once I got in the back of the truck, I looked out the window at Dank speaking dramatically to his flunkies, who were circled around him. I just shook my head from side to side as Payback drove off.

Malik D. Rice

Chapter 33

I was on the stage with Princess Demy performing a song we collaborated on. It had hit number one on the charts and had been there for weeks. It was the hottest song in the country, and our fans were loving it.

Fifteen thousand people went bananas in the crowd as we performed the duo. Demy sang her verse while I swayed along to the beat having an out-of-body experience.

I finally made it out of the gutter! I finally accomplished all my dreams!

It came time for me to perform my verse, and I performed well for my fans giving them lots of energy and attention. Halfway through the verse, a burst of fire exploded in the background, and the fans became more frantic with amazement.

I tried to continue my verse, but the heat from the fire was becoming more and more unbearable by the second. I turned my back to the crowd to see the fire. It had gotten out of control, and it was getting closer. Coming straight my way.

"Get the fuck up nigga!" Donny barked loudly while pulling me off the bed from my feet.

Thump!

My head hit the carpeted floor hard, waking me up straight out of my sleep.

"What the fuckkkkk!" I bellowed as my eyes popped open, and I was snapped back to reality.

My fucking room was on fire. Wild flames came from the wall, making its way to my bed and anything else that got in its way.

I stood openmouthed in disbelief at the sight until Donny yanked my arm with a surprising force. I almost tripped, but thankfully I caught my footing and fell in line behind Donny.

We ran through the trailer at full speed as flames continued to flare. It wasn't just my room. The *whole* damn trailer was on fire.

"Bring yo' ass on, man!" Donny commanded firmly before kicking the front door off the hinges with two gorilla kicks.

The door flew open clearing the way for us to make a quick exit, and we did just that. It wasn't until we got outside, and my bare feet touched the cold ground, that I realized I only had on a thermal pajama set.

I automatically thought about all the clothes I left inside, then my whole stomach dropped, and anxiety hit me hard, when I remembered the Timberland shoebox under my bed, with just over forty thousand dollars inside.

I took off running back towards the trailer without a word. I already had all my chains on my neck, so all I had to do was grab the shoe box, fuck everything else.

"Hmphhhh!" Donny grunted loudly as he collided with me. He tackled me onto the ground before I could make it to the stairs. "What the fuck wrong with you man!"

"Forty thousand up under the bed nigga! We need that!" I pushed him off of me and tried to get back to my feet.

He tackled me back onto the ground. "Ain't nothing in that muthafuckin' house worth you dying for! I'm not about to let you risk yo' life for that lil shit."

I lifted my head up and watched as the flames ate through the trailer like it was nothing. I could now see the inside of the living room lit up in flames. There was a debate on if I could make it to my room, but I definitely wouldn't make it back out. Donny was right. It wasn't worth risking my life for. Forty thousand was chump change to me now.

Donny helped me up onto my feet after a few moments passed, and I began to shiver as my adrenaline began to come down. "Tell me you got the keys to the truck in them pants," I asked praying he did.

"Fucking right!" he answered while leading the way to the truck at the top of the driveway.

We'd been sitting inside of the truck, down the street from our trailer, with the heat blasting for the past five minutes. It was four o'clock in the morning. It was a long five minutes for me because so many thoughts had already crossed my mind, and more were on the way.

While Donny sat there watching the fire truck speed down the road leading to our trailer, I sat there evaluating the entire situation and plotting my next move.

It was obviously a warning message because they could've easily shot the shit up if they wanted to. More than likely, it was Dizzy or one of his minions. Venom's whole camp dealt with Dizzy personally, so their loyalty ran deeper for him than it did Venom, which is why Redd put his claws into Dizzy. It was genius on Redd's behalf because Dizzy was one helluva opponent.

I couldn't figure out a way to beat him. His team was too ruthless and way too close. They lived like Mexicans and thought like Italians. Venom created a small army of monsters, who were now trying to destroy him.

I couldn't help but shake my head from side to side and sigh out of frustration.

"Yeah, I know. I feel the same fuckin' way. Dizzy gon' get his one of these days... And look at these niggas here! Where the fuck was their antennas when muthafuckas was setting our shit on fire?" Donny asked sourly while gazing at Antonio and a few of his soldiers. They were approaching the scene from the other section of the trailer park, where the smaller trailers sat.

Antonio broke out into a run towards the trailer with his soldiers in tow. "Look at these niggas, bruh!" said Donny before turning towards me. "You know what? I wouldn't be surprised if these niggas had something to do with it in some kind of way."

"Come on now," I challenged while looking at Donny with a knowing look. "You *know* Antonio ain't no nigga like that. He definitely too loyal to switch sides bruh. You were right the first time. Dizzy got to get it. He a *real* problem these days."

I watched Antonio standing outside of the perimeter of the police tape, causing a scene. I could see things beginning to get out of hand, so I rolled my window down and stuck my head out. "Yoooo, Tonio'!"

He looked my way, squinted, and started smiling as soon as recognition hit. He jogged over to the truck. "Mannnnn, I swear I thought y'all niggas was Kentucky Fried Chicken in that muthafucka!" he informed with much relief showing on his face and in his voice as he spoke to me on the other side of the passenger's window.

"We almost was... Anyway, hold it down out here. You in charge of YF out here. Fuck Chase Gang! If a nigga is not YF, he not yo' concern. I'll be in touch. Everything is business as usual," I said before shaking Antonio's hand through the window and telling Donny to pull off.

I took a good look at my burning trailer as we rode past and came to the conclusion that I would *never* lay my head in The Chase again. It was too open, meaning too many ways the enemy could strike from. I needed a safe spot.

I needed a lot at the moment. We had to start over, but it could've been worse. A nigga could've been dead.

Chapter 34

After leaving The Chase, we headed straight for Donny's mother's house, where we grabbed some of our old clothes and stash money, before dipping back out. He wasn't on the best terms with his mother any more than I was, and the funny part is that they were the best of friends.

"We've been in this empty lot for hours. The sun is up and all. What's the move? We going to Rondo's house, a hotel, the tire shop, what? We can't just sit here all damn day; I know that for sure." Donny asked while laying back in his reclined seat.

Both of our seats were reclined. I looked over at him. "We about to get a hotel because I don't even feel like hearing Rondo's mouth right now... I'm just trying to gather all my thoughts."

"Nigga, you can gather yo' thoughts in a nice hotel. This ain't gon' cut it right here."

I sighed as I lifted my seat, so I could see out of the windshield. "Alright, drive then."

"That's the whole point bruh! Fuck all that defense shit. We basically sitting around waiting for them niggas to do something to us. That's crazy. We need to hit back," Donny debated logically.

We checked into a decent hotel down the street from the hospital Venom stayed in, after hitting the mall for some fly gear. I laid back on my bed, looking at the ceiling with my hands behind my head and my feet crossed.

Right now, I was just letting him vent because he obviously had a lot on his chest, he felt like getting off. "I understand why you on the shit you on, but you got to think about the soldiers. They not in the same boat as us, so they not thinking like that... Shit way too hectic in these streets right now to be showing weakness of any kind. If our soldiers don't feel safe under our roof, they gon' go move somewhere they do." He sat up on the edge of his bed looking over at me.

"What you want us to do then Donny?" I asked to see his vision.

He shook his head in disagreement. "Nah, not us. Let me handle the nitty-gritty shit out here. You can just lay low in here, or at Rondo house, or something."

I knew how to fight, and even bussed a shot, or two, throughout my time in the streets, but Donny knew like I knew that I was no killer. Plus, I was the head of the body, so there was no need for me to be in the field like that. I agreed with that, but I had a better idea about my whereabouts during the war.

I got up and sat up on the edge of the bed. I recently bought two YF chains to go with my DG chain. One was bigger than the other. I unclasped the bigger one and tossed it over to, Donny, who caught it in his hand.

"What's this for?" he asked confusingly.

"It's for you, nigga. Go out there and handle that business. Show them niggas why we're not to be fucked with."

Chapter 35

The next day, I sat in the backyard of a Beverly Hills mansion enjoying the warm sunshine down on my tattooed body. Ronte was hosting a pool party, and I was openmouthed.

When I called him and told him I was trying to lay low out of town, he told me he was going to fly me out to California, to a *little* pool party. The party was far from little. There were only about seventy people in attendance, but at least thirty of them were big-time celebrities.

DG Rell was definitely one of them. He started DG Records with Dinero and signed himself as an artist. His first year in the game, he won a Grammy and went triple platinum. He was the highest-paid artist on DG Records' roster, and Ronte was a close second. They were the faces of Dilluminati, and I was honored to be sitting, and eating, at the same table as them.

"You a'ight youngin'? Let me find out that Moon Rock got you too high stuck like that," Fifty asked jokingly, drawing laughter from everyone else. He was Ronte's right-hand-man, and he was alright with me.

I broke out of my trance and looked up at Fifty with an involuntary smile. I was stressing when I pulled up, so when I saw Ronte drop a half-pound on the table, I went overboard not knowing that these niggas smoked on a whole different level than I was used to.

I was high to the point where I was having an out of body experience. I had to grab a hold of reality and gain control over myself because I was making a first impression on a lot of important people, so I had to get right. "Hell yeah, nigga! Y'all got to sell me a few pounds of that shit there."

"The young nigga got to be a player because he done snatched up Princess Demy's bougie ass already. He ain't even got a deal yet!" Rell added in his thick New York accent.

I smiled harder, probably looking like Ronald McDonald. "Nahhh, we just cool."

"The bitch text your phone?" he asked with a raised eyebrow.

I nodded my head up-and-down.

"You got herrrr! I'm telling you lil' bro'! She done turned down me *and* Ronte already. I guess she like young niggas," Rell joked while laughing at his own joke.

He was a pretty boy, with a foreign nationality, and silky long hair. All the women wanted him, so for Demy to turn him down told me a lot about her. She liked what she liked.

"I see you got jokes, huh?" I countered playfully. "She a'ight though. It ain't nothing serious."

I wasn't worried about my problems back home, or nothing at the moment. I was chilling at a party full of millionaires, and they were my friends. My life was definitely worth something.

After the party died down, we retired into the house. There was a balcony overlooking the backyard in the guest room I was staying in. I was on the balcony watching four beautiful women clean up the backyard cheerfully. They just seemed so damn happy.

"I see you out here admiring my bitches." Ronte snuck up on me from behind.

I jumped a little from surprise, but quickly recovered. "All four of them yours?" I asked with interest. Ronte was real over the top and lived a real Rockstar lifestyle.

He came and leaned on the rail of the balcony next to me. "Yuuuup! I stamped all four of them personally and met them individually. They all stay and take care of this house for me and I give 'em a discount on rent... But fuck all that, What you gon' do about that situation around yo' way? I feel like you too hands-on out there. You're young, but you a boss now, and you got to start acting like it."

I shrugged my shoulders. "What I'm supposed to do? You know how shit goes in the streets. Got to claw yo' way up out of there... I got it all under control though. It's all good, big bruh."

"Nahh, I don't like the thought of that. Fuck what Rondo saying. I'm gon' get you a deal for at least $500,000, and you gon' have to get yo ass off them streets. I'm gon' set you up with a condo in Atlanta too. That gift is on me though. You got too much potential to be wasting in the streets," Ronte stated matter-a-factly.

I stood there looking up at Ronte with a blank face. "For real?"

"You know I don't do no playing. I already talked to Rondo about it and all, so it's official... I'm your new Underboss now. You don't answer to Rondo anymore because I'm marking you a Don right now. You can lay low out here for a few days. The girls are gon' take good care of you. I got a private jet to catch, lil' nigga. Take it easy," Ronte informed before taking off one of his L4E chains, passing it to me, and walking off without another word.

I looked away from him, and down at the sparkling chain in my palm. I felt a sense of relief wash over my body. I didn't have a million, but half of it was good enough. I had to get out of them streets. I couldn't let a nigga kill me.

I was a made-man now. I was Don Manny.

Chapter 36

I ended up staying in Beverly Hills for a few days. Ronte's girls made sure I was straight like he said, and I enjoyed myself. They took me out to different places, and I saw a lot of new things for the first time. I didn't really want to go, but I had unfinished business back in my city before I moved to Atlanta.

The only thing material I had in Rondoville was my stash buried in the dirt behind Donny's mother's house, but that's not all I was going back for. I was going back for Donny himself. I promised to take him all the way to the top with me, and that's what I meant.

I told him to meet me at the hotel, so I could talk to him about some serious shit. I walked in on him watching TV while smoking a joint of weed. "Man, put that shit out fool. I got some shit that's gon' put you on yo' ass," I greeted with a big smile.

The Moon Rock put Donny on his ass just like I promised. I took the train back, just so I could bring the two pounds of weed Ronte gave me.

"Yoooo! This shit got me floating nigga! Shitttt!" Donny exclaimed excitedly.

I released a thick cloud of smoke through my nose smoothly. "Yeahhh. This that real rapper weed, nigga. This all we gon' be smoking from now on."

"What you needed to talk to me about though bruh? I told you we hit back at them niggas. Shot up their whole apartments twice since you've been gone. They gon' learn about this shit," he informed proudly with his chest out and chin up.

I nodded slowly in approval. "I ain't never doubt you. I knew you were gon' handle businesses that's why I gave you that chain before I left... but on some real shit, you don't got to worry about that no more because we done finally made it up out this shit, man."

He looked at me sideways. "What? Made it out how?"

I told him all about the deal and made-man stripes Ronte gave me, and the big condo in Atlanta. "All we got to do is dig that money up and hit the road."

I was expecting a few cheers, a smile, or something to come up out of him, but Donny didn't do any of that. He just nodded his head up-and-down slowly. "Bruh, you know I'm happy for you and I think you need to go for it. You *wayyyy* bigger than these here streets, but me? I'm made for this shit. I wouldn't be happy in the industry. It ain't for me, but it's definitely for you, my nigga."

I looked at Donny like he'd grew another nose. "You serious right now? I got you a one-way ticket out of the hood, and you turn it down? Like, for real?"

"Yeah, man. You can focus on rapping and all that other legal shit you trying to do with YF. I'm gon' hang back and hold the trap down. Somebody got to keep the drug money flowing for us. Just plug me in with Rondo before you leave and let him know he can trust me. That's what you can do for me."

My nigga was right. He was built for the streets, and I couldn't really blame him for wanting to stay and hold shit down. At least I would have somebody I could trust running YF on the streets. "Aight, say less. You got the key to the streets, my nigga."

"DG," he said instead of saying *I love you.*

I shook his hand. "L4E," I responded instead of saying *I love you too.*

TO BE CONTINUED...
Money, Murder & Memories 2
Coming Soon

Submission Guideline

Submit the first three chapters of your completed manuscript to ldpsubmissions@gmail.com, subject line: Your book's title. The manuscript must be in a .doc file and sent as an attachment. Document should be in Times New Roman, double spaced and in size 12 font. Also, provide your synopsis and full contact information. If sending multiple submissions, they must each be in a separate email.

Have a story but no way to send it electronically? You can still submit to LDP/Ca$h Presents. Send in the first three chapters, written or typed, of your completed manuscript to:

LDP: Submissions Dept
Po Box 944
Stockbridge, Ga 30281

DO NOT send original manuscript. Must be a duplicate.

Provide your synopsis and a cover letter containing your full contact information.

Thanks for considering LDP and Ca$h Presents.

Malik D. Rice

BOW DOWN TO MY GANGSTA

By **Ca$h**

TORN BETWEEN TWO

By **Coffee**

THE STREETS STAINED MY SOUL **II**

By **Marcellus Allen**

BLOOD OF A BOSS **VI**

SHADOWS OF THE GAME II

By **Askari**

LOYAL TO THE GAME **IV**

By **T.J. & Jelissa**

IF LOVING YOU IS WRONG… **III**

By **Jelissa**

TRUE SAVAGE **VIII**

MIDNIGHT CARTEL III

DOPE BOY MAGIC IV

CITY OF KINGZ II

By **Chris Green**

BLAST FOR ME **III**

A SAVAGE DOPEBOY III

CUTTHROAT MAFIA III

DUFFLE BAG CARTEL VI

By **Ghost**

A HUSTLER'S DECEIT III

KILL ZONE **II**

BAE BELONGS TO ME III

A DOPE BOY'S QUEEN III

By **Aryanna**

COKE KINGS V

KING OF THE TRAP II

By **T.J. Edwards**

GORILLAZ IN THE BAY V

3X KRAZY II

De'Kari

THE STREETS ARE CALLING II

Duquie Wilson

KINGPIN KILLAZ IV

STREET KINGS III

PAID IN BLOOD III

CARTEL KILLAZ IV

DOPE GODS III

Hood Rich

SINS OF A HUSTLA II

ASAD

KINGZ OF THE GAME VI

Playa Ray

SLAUGHTER GANG IV

RUTHLESS HEART IV

By Willie Slaughter

THE HEART OF A SAVAGE III

By Jibril Williams

FUK SHYT II

By Blakk Diamond

THE REALEST KILLAZ III

By Tranay Adams

TRAP GOD III

By Troublesome

YAYO IV

GHOST MOB

Stilloan Robinson

KINGPIN DREAMS III

By Paper Boi Rari

CREAM II

By Yolanda Moore

SON OF A DOPE FIEND III

By Renta

FOREVER GANGSTA II

GLOCKS ON SATIN SHEETS III

By Adrian Dulan

LOYALTY AIN'T PROMISED III

By Keith Williams

THE PRICE YOU PAY FOR LOVE II

By Destiny Skai

CONFESSIONS OF A GANGSTA III

By Nicholas Lock

I'M NOTHING WITHOUT HIS LOVE II

SINS OF A THUG II

By Monet Dragun

LIFE OF A SAVAGE IV

MURDA SEASON IV

GANGLAND CARTEL III

By **Romell Tukes**

QUIET MONEY IV

THUG LIFE II

By **Trai'Quan**

THE STREETS MADE ME III

By **Larry D. Wright**

THE ULTIMATE SACRIFICE VI

IF YOU CROSS ME ONCE II

ANGEL III

By **Anthony Fields**

FRIEND OR FOE III

By **Mimi**

SAVAGE STORMS II

By **Meesha**

BLOOD ON THE MONEY II

By J-Blunt

THE STREETS WILL NEVER CLOSE II

By K'ajji

NIGHTMARES OF A HUSTLA II

By King Dream

THE WIFEY I USED TO BE II

By Nicole Goosby

IN THE ARM OF HIS BOSS

By Jamila

MONEY, MURDER & MEMORIES II

Malik D. Rice

Available Now

RESTRAINING ORDER **I & II**

By **CA$H & Coffee**

LOVE KNOWS NO BOUNDARIES **I II & III**

By **Coffee**

RAISED AS A GOON I, II, III & IV

BRED BY THE SLUMS I, II, III

BLAST FOR ME I & II

ROTTEN TO THE CORE I II III

A BRONX TALE I, II, III

DUFFLE BAG CARTEL I II III IV V

HEARTLESS GOON I II III IV

A SAVAGE DOPEBOY I II

HEARTLESS GOON I II III

DRUG LORDS I II III

CUTTHROAT MAFIA I II

By **Ghost**

LAY IT DOWN **I & II**

LAST OF A DYING BREED

BLOOD STAINS OF A SHOTTA I & II III

By **Jamaica**

LOYAL TO THE GAME I II III

LIFE OF SIN I, II III

By **TJ & Jelissa**

BLOODY COMMAS I & II

SKI MASK CARTEL I II & III

KING OF NEW YORK I II,III IV V

RISE TO POWER I II III

COKE KINGS I II III IV

BORN HEARTLESS I II III IV

KING OF THE TRAP

By **T.J. Edwards**

IF LOVING HIM IS WRONG…I & II

LOVE ME EVEN WHEN IT HURTS I II III

By **Jelissa**

WHEN THE STREETS CLAP BACK I & II III

THE HEART OF A SAVAGE I II

By **Jibril Williams**

A DISTINGUISHED THUG STOLE MY HEART I II & III

Money, Murder & Memories

LOVE SHOULDN'T HURT I II III IV

RENEGADE BOYS I II III IV

PAID IN KARMA I II III

SAVAGE STORMS

By **Meesha**

A GANGSTER'S CODE I &, II III

A GANGSTER'S SYN I II III

THE SAVAGE LIFE I II III

CHAINED TO THE STREETS I II III

BLOOD ON THE MONEY

By J-Blunt

PUSH IT TO THE LIMIT

By **Bre' Hayes**

BLOOD OF A BOSS **I, II, III, IV, V**

SHADOWS OF THE GAME

By **Askari**

THE STREETS BLEED MURDER **I, II & III**

THE HEART OF A GANGSTA I II& III

By **Jerry Jackson**

CUM FOR ME I II III IV V VI

An **LDP Erotica Collaboration**

BRIDE OF A HUSTLA **I II & II**

THE FETTI GIRLS **I, II& III**

CORRUPTED BY A GANGSTA I, II III, IV

BLINDED BY HIS LOVE

THE PRICE YOU PAY FOR LOVE

DOPE GIRL MAGIC I II III

By **Destiny Skai**

WHEN A GOOD GIRL GOES BAD

By **Adrienne**

Malik D. Rice

THE COST OF LOYALTY I II III
By Kweli
A GANGSTER'S REVENGE **I II III & IV**
THE BOSS MAN'S DAUGHTERS I II III IV V
A SAVAGE LOVE **I & II**
BAE BELONGS TO ME I II
A HUSTLER'S DECEIT I, II, III
WHAT BAD BITCHES DO I, II, III
SOUL OF A MONSTER I II III
KILL ZONE
A DOPE BOY'S QUEEN I II
By **Aryanna**
A KINGPIN'S AMBITON
A KINGPIN'S AMBITION **II**
I MURDER FOR THE DOUGH
By **Ambitious**
TRUE SAVAGE I II III IV V VI VII
DOPE BOY MAGIC I, II, III
MIDNIGHT CARTEL I II
CITY OF KINGZ
By **Chris Green**
A DOPEBOY'S PRAYER
By **Eddie "Wolf" Lee**
THE KING CARTEL **I, II & III**
By **Frank Gresham**
THESE NIGGAS AIN'T LOYAL **I, II & III**
By **Nikki Tee**
GANGSTA SHYT **I II &III**
By **CATO**
THE ULTIMATE BETRAYAL

Money, Murder & Memories

By **Phoenix**

BOSS'N UP **I , II & III**

By **Royal Nicole**

I LOVE YOU TO DEATH

By Destiny J

I RIDE FOR MY HITTA

I STILL RIDE FOR MY HITTA

By **Misty Holt**

LOVE & CHASIN' PAPER

By **Qay Crockett**

TO DIE IN VAIN

SINS OF A HUSTLA

By **ASAD**

BROOKLYN HUSTLAZ

By **Boogsy Morina**

BROOKLYN ON LOCK I & II

By **Sonovia**

GANGSTA CITY

By **Teddy Duke**

A DRUG KING AND HIS DIAMOND I & II III

A DOPEMAN'S RICHES

HER MAN, MINE'S TOO I, II

CASH MONEY HO'S

THE WIFEY I USED TO BE

By Nicole Goosby

TRAPHOUSE KING **I II & III**

KINGPIN KILLAZ I II III

STREET KINGS I II

PAID IN BLOOD **I II**

CARTEL KILLAZ I II III

Malik D. Rice

DOPE GODS I II

By **Hood Rich**

LIPSTICK KILLAH **I, II, III**

CRIME OF PASSION I II & III

FRIEND OR FOE I II

By **Mimi**

STEADY MOBBN' **I, II, III**

THE STREETS STAINED MY SOUL

By **Marcellus Allen**

WHO SHOT YA **I, II, III**

SON OF A DOPE FIEND I II

Renta

GORILLAZ IN THE BAY **I II III IV**

TEARS OF A GANGSTA I II

3X KRAZY

DE'KARI

TRIGGADALE I II III

Elijah R. Freeman

GOD BLESS THE TRAPPERS I, II, III

THESE SCANDALOUS STREETS I, II, III

FEAR MY GANGSTA I, II, III IV, V

THESE STREETS DON'T LOVE NOBODY I, II

BURY ME A G I, II, III, IV, V

A GANGSTA'S EMPIRE I, II, III, IV

THE DOPEMAN'S BODYGAURD I II

THE REALEST KILLAZ I II

Tranay Adams

THE STREETS ARE CALLING

Duquie Wilson

MARRIED TO A BOSS... I II III

184

Money, Murder & Memories

By Destiny Skai & Chris Green

KINGZ OF THE GAME I II III IV V

Playa Ray

SLAUGHTER GANG I II III

RUTHLESS HEART I II III

By Willie Slaughter

FUK SHYT

By Blakk Diamond

DON'T F#CK WITH MY HEART I II

By Linnea

ADDICTED TO THE DRAMA I II III

IN THE ARM OF HIS BOSS II

By Jamila

YAYO I II III

A SHOOTER'S AMBITION I II

By S. Allen

TRAP GOD I II

By Troublesome

FOREVER GANGSTA

GLOCKS ON SATIN SHEETS I II

By Adrian Dulan

TOE TAGZ I II III

By Ah'Million

KINGPIN DREAMS I II

By Paper Boi Rari

CONFESSIONS OF A GANGSTA I II

By Nicholas Lock

I'M NOTHING WITHOUT HIS LOVE

SINS OF A THUG

By Monet Dragun

Malik D. Rice

CAUGHT UP IN THE LIFE I II III
By Robert Baptiste
NEW TO MONEY, MURDER & MEMORIES
THE GAME I II III
By **Malik D. Rice**
LIFE OF A SAVAGE I II III
A GANGSTA'S QUR'AN I II III
MURDA SEASON I II III
GANGLAND CARTEL I II
By **Romell Tukes**
LOYALTY AIN'T PROMISED I II
By Keith Williams
QUIET MONEY I II III
THUG LIFE
By **Trai'Quan**
THE STREETS MADE ME I II
By **Larry D. Wright**
THE ULTIMATE SACRIFICE I, II, III, IV, V
KHADIFI
IF YOU CROSS ME ONCE
ANGEL I II
By **Anthony Fields**
THE LIFE OF A HOOD STAR
By Ca$h & Rashia Wilson
THE STREETS WILL NEVER CLOSE
By K'ajji
CREAM
By Yolanda Moore
NIGHTMARES OF A HUSTLA
By King Dream

186

BOOKS BY LDP'S CEO, CA$H

TRUST IN NO MAN

TRUST IN NO MAN 2

TRUST IN NO MAN 3

BONDED BY BLOOD

SHORTY GOT A THUG

THUGS CRY

THUGS CRY 2

THUGS CRY 3

TRUST NO BITCH

TRUST NO BITCH 2

TRUST NO BITCH 3

TIL MY CASKET DROPS

RESTRAINING ORDER

RESTRAINING ORDER 2

IN LOVE WITH A CONVICT

LIFE OF A HOOD STAR

Malik D. Rice

CPSIA information can be obtained
at www.ICGtesting.com
Printed in the USA
LVHW021643170121
676729LV00013B/1637